Lloyd Stevens Bryce

Friends in Exile

A Tale of Diplomacy, Coronets, and Hearts

Lloyd Stevens Bryce

Friends in Exile
A Tale of Diplomacy, Coronets, and Hearts

ISBN/EAN: 9783744673570

Printed in Europe, USA, Canada, Australia, Japan

Cover: Foto ©Andreas Hilbeck / pixelio.de

More available books at **www.hansebooks.com**

FRIENDS IN EXILE.

A TALE OF

DIPLOMACY, CORONETS AND HEARTS.

BY

LLOYD BRYCE,

*Author of "Paradise," "The Romance of an Alter Ego," "A
Dream of Conquest," "Lady Blanche's Salon," etc.*

F. TENNYSON NEELY,

PUBLISHER,

114

FIFTH AVENUE,

CHICAGO.   NEW YORK.   LONDON.

CONTENTS.

FRIENDS IN EXILE.

I.

MR. JACKSON SECURES A GREAT DIPLOMATIC PLUM.

"There's no use in taking it, Samuel. It's only a waste of room," and a matronly looking woman of fifty dubiously surveyed the choked condition of sundry trunks and portmanteaus that lay scattered around her.

"Put it in, Martha, put it in," replied her husband. "Old coats, like old friends, are not to be discarded."

"But you have long been needing a new dress coat, and when you get to Paris, you can buy one of a later cut. Now let me take it and give it away to one of my pensioners."

"Martha, I've worn that coat during the best part of my public career, and what's good enough for the White House ought to be good enough for foreign courts," and a look of resolution, before which his opponents had often quailed, softened to a smile as he added: "Besides, I have a sentiment for that coat, for I wore it at our silver wedding fully fifteen years ago. Under the circumstances, I should think you would be the last to bid me throw it away."

"Very well, then, Samuel, that settles the matter—we will take it," and the coat was deposited in one of the many portmanteaus. A long silence followed, during which the lady continued the packing— her husband the while walking up and down the room with his hands in his trousers' pockets.

It was a large, commodious apartment of a large, commodious house, furnished with that old-time primness which has an attractiveness quite its own. All spoke of comfort; the huge four-poster bedstead and the mahogany chest of drawers and wardrobes; while the exquisite tidiness everywhere gave evidence of the house-wifely qualities of the mistress. For **Mr.**

Jackson was fortunate both in his marriage and in his career. As a lawyer he had reached the bench by thirty-seven, he had served several terms in both houses of Congress, and finally, the ambassador to France, passing to an equally pleasant post, let us hope, in another world, Mr. Jackson had been given the vacant place.

Here, however, he was to encounter conditions for which with all his success he was little prepared. The world of fashion, of art, of literature, as well as of French politics, in short the great world of Paris, were to him as a sealed book. Yet his qualms less concerned the future than the past.

Pausing in his restless walk, he resumed: "The way things have turned out, I have but one cause of irritation, Martha, and that's the noise the papers are making over a speech I made two years ago in the senate."

"What was it you said, Samuel?"

"Well, more than I intended. It was over the debate about these very embassies. I alluded to them with contempt, advocated republican simplicity, ridiculed any aping of European forms and ceremonies, and further, I closed with an amendment to abolish the whole diplomatic service."

"It's certainly very awkward, Samuel." your having made such a speech."

"And I cannot help asking myself," continued the gentleman, "how I am to satisfy my conscience in accepting this post after saying what I did ?"

"But why did you not think of that speech when you allowed your name to be urged for the appointment ?"

"The fact is, I had quite forgotten it, though now it rises up, like a ghost, to cast an imputation on my sincerity."

"I imagine your reputation for sincerity is proof against what the press can say; besides, the more one set of papers attacks you, the more the other will rally to your support."

"Oh, it's not that they're not rallying to my support—quite the contrary; it's whether, with this speech in my mind, I deserve all the encomiums they're lavishing upon me. That's my dilemma. Indeed, I really think that speech has popularized me enormously with the country at large."

"If that be the case, I would let the matter stand as an offset to the number of times you've been misrepresented by the press."

Her husband seemed relieved.

"That's the way I argue myself," he replied. "At all events, it's too late to worry over it now, and I have this to console me, that one of my speeches at least has been unearthed from the Record— that repository of defunct utterances, and which for oblivion, it is said, outrivals the fly-leaf of a hotel Bible."

Judge Jackson's intimation as to the approval of the country at his appointment was not exaggerated. Deep down in the people's heart was a feeling—if not voiced, yet strong all the same—that these great diplomatic positions had been too long held as the peculiar belonging of a select few; and that however great might have been the abilities, and however distinguished the services of his predecessors, a departure ought to be made by giving to a man distinctly in touch with the masses an occasional chance of filling such a position. Judge Jackson, in spite of a handsome fortune, a large house, and a liberal hospitality, happened, for the moment, to meet this conception. No one could aver that his successes in life had affected the natural simplicity of his manner, his innate kindliness, or his quaint humor; but, without any other claim to being distinctly one of the people than a speech he now repented making, he suddenly found himself a popular hero. Nor was anyone more surprised than he at the peculiar character of the discussion elicited by his appointment; but, being a prudent man, he confided his doubts only to his wife, and these satisfied, repaired to his post with a promptness which might have argued a determination of reaching it before a turn in the public sentiment could come.

II.

"Paris! Paris! Paris! Tout le monde descend de voiture," shouted the railroad guard, opening wide the door of the Calais-Douvre train, on its arrival at its terminus one morning. Among the passengers who obeyed this summons were our new representative and his wife.

What a revelation that first glimpse of Paris is to the stranger! What a world it seems with its orderly rush and bustle—with its air of luxury and the conspicuous absence of the commercial element. Then its cleanliness and its beauty, too! Why, the very trees look as if they were combed and brushed each morning. All here seems ordered so as to make life a pleasure, and that grim puritanism which faces every innocent joy with a forbidding "Thou Shalt Not" is consigned to a deserved Coventry.

These reflections passed through the

mind of Mr. Jackson, while seated on the top of a hotel omnibus where, to the secret chagrin of the secretary of the embassy, he had insisted on climbing; for this offi-cial had come to meet his new chief at the station, and was occupying the interior with Mrs. Jackson.

A word as to Mr. Pettigrew. The secret spring of the secretary's every action was pride in the American Embassy. Per-haps he was a formalist—perhaps a stickler for etiquette, but to maintain the dignity of the embassy in the eyes of the European world, if not to have it outshine all other embassies and legations, was the object of his life.

To the attainment of this end, as it will be seen later on, there was no sacri-fice which he was not willing to make.

Mr. Pettigrew had already broken in several superiors at other posts and recognizing the importance of early acquiring the good will of Mr. Jackson, he made quick to meet him at the station. Moreover, he collected his luggage, saw that it was duly consigned to the

temporary quarters selected for the new-
comers, and further made himself as
agreeable and affable as lay in his
power. Yet our envoy failed to do justice to the motives of his subordinate.
There seemed an artificiality about his
politeness, as if it did not emanate from
the heart. He disliked, too, the cut of his
whiskers, the way they were brushed forward, and particularly did he dislike the
little mustache and imperial that ornamented his upper and lower lips. Until
now, he could scarcely have imagined that
such trivial matters could affect him so
disagreeably. Besides, he thought he
detected in his very deference an air of
patronage, almost of condescension, that
seemed to say, "Behold in me the perfect diplomat; put yourself in my hands
and I will in time turn you out like me."
Mr. Pettigrew must be taken down at
once, and to confess the truth, Mr. Jackson's purpose in mounting to the box was
as much to mark his sense of independence
as to obtain the favorable view of the city
which that position afforded.

III.

THE ADVENT OF MRS. ASHER THE DIVINE.

It is the delightful hour of half after five, when the prospect of an eight o'clock dinner just begins to gladden the atmosphere, and tea as an interlude comes to soothe the weary march of time.

Imagine an apartment, small, to be sure, but crowded both with people and bric-a-brac. On a divan, like a queen surrounded by her satellites, reclines the hostess, and—an occurrence so rare that it deserves special mention—her husband has the floor; for, as a general rule, Mr. de Trow is kept in the background by his wife.

"But it is true, quite true," he was saying. "You could have knocked me down with a feather." Then for the third time he described the entrance of Mr. Jackson on the box of the omnibus. "You see, I happened to be down near the station as the party were driving away; but, though Pettigrew had told me that he was expecting his new chief, I could never have realized that he would be on the outside of a hotel omnibus."

"Why not? I always sit there when I get the chance," said a tall young English diplomat. "Much more comfortable than inside with one's wife."

"Do you really take that view of it?" inquired Mr. de Trow. "Well, perhaps you're right after all; only it struck me as a little odd."

"What was his wife like?" inquired a bright-eyed little woman, whose bird-like appearance was enhanced by a scarf of feathers about her neck.

"To judge from the glimpse I had of her, she seemed a rather handsome woman," admitted Mr. de Trow, "quiet and dignified-looking."

"I hope they will prove people of the world, like our last ambassador and his wife," murmured Mrs. de Trow. "That is the first essential."

"I don't see why they didn't appoint Pettigrew," said Mr. de Trow. "In my opinion he would make an ideal——"

The conversation was interrupted by the entrance of a dark-bearded young man. "But I've found her," he exclaimed impulsively, "I've found her at last. Congratulate me, ladies," and he advanced and kissed Mrs. de Trow's hand.

" Who is it that you have found ? " asked Mrs. de Trow, with languid interest.

" Why, she of whom I have so frequently spoken to you all lately. She is a compatriot of yours," and the new arrival, who, because he came from Sardinia, was known to the English-speaking colony as Sardines, took his seat on the divan alongside of the hostess.

" But we have so many compatriots here," complained Mrs. de Trow. " What might her name be ? I suppose she rejoices in one."

" Ah ! her name—*diable !*—your English names—Ashere—Ashard—It is like that. But she is divine, and she has wealth ; she owns the gold mines of the Rocky Mountains, ten thousand slaves, too, of the African race, all in her own right."

" But you have abolished negro slavery,

haven't you, to make yourselves the slaves of the Irish?" laughed the English diplomat, as he turned to the hostess. "At least they seemed to run all your towns and legislatures when I was in the States."

"Yes; we adopted the Irish when we turned the English out," replied Mrs. de Trow tartly, "and, on the whole, I think we have benefited by the change."

"Bravo!" laughed the Britisher good-humoredly; "but I must admit you atone for your severity to us in the past by your hospitality to us now. Never had such a good time in my life as a month I once passed at Newport."

"Ah! Newpore—Newpore—Newpore is divine!" exclaimed the exuberant Sardinian. "At Newpore one dreams!"

"I should say, rather, one dines," replied the Englishman. "More dinners in a week than during the whole London season. By the way, though, Sardines, this mythical lady you were telling us about—is she a widow?"

"She dresses in black, and seems to mourn," said the Sardinian plaintively.

"That settles it," was the Englishman's stolid reply. "But one more question— was it at Newport that you first met her?"

"No, it was at Nice. She had just re-turned from a trip up the Nile. Now she has come to inhabit Paris."

"The question, therefore, is whether she is respectable," put in an American duch-ess.

"Or visitable," put in an American princess.

"Ah, yes, that is the question," replied an American countess; and the conversa-tion drifted off as conversations do, yet always kept returning to the female Monte Cristo.

It argues a certain gift in a person that she becomes the subject of this kind of interest. If you doubt the assertion, observe your own circle of acquaintance; notice how many are striving after such recognition, and how few succeed. Yes, it requires talent to become the talk even of a small place; but to become the talk of Paris requires genius. Recent as had been her advent here, Mrs. Asher was on the edge of this distinction. She was just beginning to be talked about; and, inasmuch as everything about her was exaggerated, the beginning might be called auspicious. Curiosity was titillated, too, by the fact that as yet no one could tell whether she was not an adventuress of a higher order.

"But I assure you she is of great consideration in her own land," continued the Sardinian, "and I predict that you will not only be meeting her before long in the world, but that you will all be crowding her *salon*."

"When that day comes I hope you will get your reward. Your *claque* will have largely assisted her," said Mrs. de Trow as she turned coldly away from the speaker. For while her curiosity was keen about this woman, she resented Signor de Maracovini's interest in her, as she considered the young man her own private property. Moreover, she resented the fact of any woman's coming to Paris to dispute her own supremacy. For Mrs. de Trow enjoyed a unique position, largely because of the originality of her conduct and the absence of anything like reticence in her conversation. Besides, she cultivated a rôle that kept the male sex, and particularly the diplomatic corps, in a continual state of ferment. She talked of the communion of two spirits, the romance of the soul, the glory of a grand passion; and, though many had learned that her professions on these tender topics were purely theoretical, they still continued their allegiance; for desertion after a certain period of devotion is a confession of failure which man's pride is not always willing to make.

On Signor de Maracovini, the suspicion was gradually beginning to dawn that she was trifling with him; but, being the latest and freshest addition to the corps, he could not submit as tamely as the rest; and, if it must be acknowledged, in his open admiration for this mysterious Mrs. Asher he was simply carrying out the policy of playing one woman against another, and of showing that, should the object of his devotion continue unappreciative, he knew where to seek consolation.

IV.

"THEY HAVE ALWAYS JUST BURIED THEIR HUSBANDS OR DROWNED THEM."

PENDING his official reception by the head of the French government, which the minister of foreign affairs had intimated would occur in a day or so, the judge repaired next morning bright and early to the embassy. Here he was met by Mr. Pettigrew; and, after a brief survey of the apartment, which consisted of an ante-chamber and several rooms, and an equally cursory initiation into the daily routine of business, he dismissed his secretary as an escort to Mrs. Jackson, who was anxious to purchase a guide book of Paris.

Thus Mr. Jackson was left alone with his letters, of which he found a large accumulation. Applications for one or other of the secretaryships largely predominated. These numbered nearly two hundred. They came from every corner of Europe whither our itinerant countrymen had wandered, and, it is needless to say, from every part of America—one being actually from a lady in Iowa, who urged her appointment on the score of the impetus it would give to the female suffrage movement in her own State. These letters Mr. Pettigrew had pigeon-holed as non-important.

Next in order were requests for presentation at the different courts in Europe; or, more properly speaking, for letters of introduction to other representatives with a view to that happy result. In the average traveler's opinion, the principal function of his minister is to place him on pleasant and easy terms of familiarity with the crowned heads of Europe.

Then there were letters seeking information on the cost of living in Paris, the price of apartments, the best and cheapest shops—one writer going so far as to request the ambassador to meet his baggage on a specified day at the station, and to hold it at the embassy till called for.

Yet another class of missives prayed him to investigate and report upon the financial condition of this American lady, or of that.

Such appeals were, for the most part, from impecunious Frenchmen.

Now, our envoy when in Congress had had a special knack in disposing of his correspondence. It might be said that his success in public life had been in no slight degree furthered by the attention he gave to his letters. He always answered them in his own hand, and was never too busy to answer them promptly. But there was much in his present correspondence that baffled him. Nor did the room or its contents furnish any inspiration. Though we have raised our ministers to ambassadors we have made no corresponding change in their official abodes. These are marked by the same stern simplicity as of yore. Consular reports filled the bookcase of the room in which Mr. Jackson sat. On the walls an engraving of Mr. Lincoln looked sadly at Mr. Hayes. A pair of crossed American flags were gracefully held in position over Mr. Jackson's desk by a brass eagle, while in a far corner a red ice-water cooler suggested thoughts of home. Yet none of these helped Mr. Jackson with his letters.

You ask, why had he not kept his secretary by him instead of sending him off with Mrs. Jackson? An ambassador wishes to show his independence of his secretary during the first few days of his career. Afterward he becomes wiser.

The day was warm—a lovely spring morning, soft and balmy, with that translucent brightness peculiar to Paris. The window was slightly open, and through the aperture came the roar of the great city. Somehow a vague feeling of loneliness stole over him. Presently there was a ring at the bell outside on the landing, followed in due course by a knock at the door and the entrance of the chief clerk of the embassy.

"Monsieur l'Ambassadeur," observed the clerk, "a lady desires to see your excellency."

"Pray admit her, Monsieur Antel, and have the kindness to leave the door open."

It was the invariable habit of our representative never to be closeted with any stranger of the opposite sex. The abrupt collapse in the political careers of two of his personal friends dated from their neg-lect of a similar caution.

A lady in mourning, and deeply veiled, entered. She was of a slight figure, with a profusion of golden hair showing beneath her bonnet.

Mr. Jackson rose as the visitor advanced.

"I wish to see the new American ambassador," she said.

Mr. Jackson bowed. "Yours to com-mand, madam," he replied with old-time courtesy.

The lady took a seat. What an art it is to do so gracefully! Some women fall upon a chair as if it were an enemy to be vanquished; others sidle into it as if they were breaking a commandment, and wished to do it surreptitiously. The visitor dropped into hers as if she were a leaf that fell from heaven.

When she raised her veil she displayed a pale, delicate beauty that was almost girlish. There was a shrinking, uncertain air about her, and her eyes had a dreamy expression as they wandered toward the window. Suddenly they seemed to fill with tears, and she pressed her handkerchief to her brow.

The judge was on his guard in a minute. The meetings that had broken his friends' careers had both begun by a woman bursting into tears.

"Monsieur Antel," discreetly called the envoy to the clerk, "please bring the lady a glass of ice water." She took it gratefully, and it seemed to restore her.

"Oh, pardon my giving way, sir," she exclaimed; "but I have gone through so much lately. You must forgive me, too, for intruding on your privacy so soon after your arrival. But I was so lonely. I felt so helpless, too, in this great, cruel capital, after my sad affliction."

"And you are in trouble?" inquired the ambassador cautiously.

"I lost my husband, barely six weeks ago, in Egypt. He was buried far away from friends and kin."

"*Gredin!*" muttered M. Antel, from behind the door, "they have always just buried their husbands—or drowned them."

"I am extremely sorry to hear it,

madam," replied Mr. Jackson sympathet·
ically. "Might I inquire the nature of his
complaint?"

"Oh, sir, I suppose I must inform you.
He had lately come into possession of a
considerable fortune. It turned his head.
His entire nature changed. From being
kind and considerate he grew cruel and
intemperate. He proved faithless to me,
too, and ended in a drunkard's grave."

There is nothing that appeals to a true
American heart, and especially to a man of
Mr. Jackson's age, like a charge by a pretty
woman against another man, though it
be her husband. The ambassador was
affected at last.

"You are highly wrought up, my young
madam. What did you say the name
was?"

"Asher—Mrs. Henry Asher."

"Henry Asher!" ejaculated Mr. Jackson
in unfeigned surprise. "Surely your husband was no relation to my young *protégé*,
Henry Asher, whom I got appointed to
West Point?"

"The same, sir."

"The same? Well, well, well! Poor Henry! I never knew he was even married, much less dead. He was the most promising youth in the public schools of Dianapolis. But why did you not mention your name to me at first?"

"It seemed like trying to establish a claim to your consideration on too slender grounds," was the reply; "at least, before informing you of his career. I thought you might not approve of his entering foreign service; for, after attaining the rank of captain in our army, he accepted a commission from the Khedive. That is how he came to die away from home; but the Egyptian phase of his life I do not care to dwell on; it is too sad, too sad."

"I was not aware of his leaving our army," said Mr. Jackson. "You see, I have lost sight of him for the last ten years or so. But how did he acquire his fortune? I should hardly conceive that campaigning in Egypt afforded many opportunities for growing rich."

"Ah, that is the question," again muttered M. Antel from his retreat.

"Assuredly the situation is becoming interesting."

"He inherited his fortune from a distant connection," answered the lady vaguely. "If he had only taken my advice and resigned, he might be alive even now. But he was wedded to the country—enjoyed the climate and the opportunity his wealth gave him for indulgence in his dissipations. Oh, sir! is it right for me to retain this fortune which proved his ruin?" she ran on. "Is it even right for me to wear these black robes for a man I had ceased to respect? Is it not a lie, sir, that I am holding out to the world?"

"Then remove the black robes, my dear young friend—I mean, substitute for them a gayer apparel," said the judge.

"Oh, thank you, sir, thank you!" she ejaculated.

"Yes," continued he oracularly, "since you ask my advice, I would suggest that you retain the fortune and discard the weeds. You see, this course has the merit of allowing of reconsideration, which the other would not."

"You do not know what comfort you have given me," replied the lady, with deep emotion. "Ever since I came here, I have been torturing myself to decide what I ought to do. When I heard of your arrival, I could not withstand the temptation of coming to learn whether the widow of your old friend, who had so inadequately repaid your kindness, could have any claim on your consideration."

The ambassador was strangely touched. At this moment the sound of steps in the corridor was followed by the appearance of Mr. Pettigrew and Mrs. Jackson.

"Madam," exclaimed the judge, turning to his wife, "I have a little surprise for you which I think will prove an agreeable one. Allow me to present to you the widow of Henry Asher. She's alone in Paris, and I am sure will appreciate your friendship."

An unspoken objection in Mr. Pettigrew's face urged on the envoy. "Perhaps you might induce her to dine with us this evening. We're all strangers alike, and she will help to cheer us up."

V.

THE VICOMTE'S BACCARAT SYSTEM AND WHAT IT LED TO.

AMONG the young men that floated from one drawing room to another of the gay Paris world, was a rather handsome Frenchman, with a jerky manner, curly hair, and a mustache with two little waxed-up points. He, too, enjoyed the reputation of being talked about, and was envied accordingly. Indeed, I might say that he was among the most envied of all the young men of his day. For had not the celebrated actress Ariane de l'Enfer allowed him the privilege of half ruining himself on her account? Again, because of his attentions to the wife of a wealthy banker, the unhappy husband was supposed to have committed suicide by hurling himself under the wheels of a Paris omnibus, though his fall was due to stepping on an orange peel. Among his lesser claims to fame were a couple of widely advertised duels; he got his boots from Thomas; and while vehemently upholding the Catholic religion, skeptically maintained that Pio Nono was less divinely inspired than Worth.

These varied distinctions, qualifications, and modes of thought, coupled with an erect bearing and ancient lineage, formed in the person of the Vicomte de Dindon a combination that, in the slang of the capital, is recognized as the *dernier ornement de la gomme.*

Ruskin has epigrammatically observed that the most marked features of modern fashionable life are occupation without object and indolence without repose. Of the truth of this saying the vicomte offered a striking illustration, although a feverish craving for excitement, which at times possessed him, was regarded by many as the restlessness of an ambition that could find no outlet, and the indolence supervening as the natural result of realizing the futility of any effort, however well-directed. For alas! belonging to the well-known family of La Vieille Roche, what prospects, they asked, could the republic extend to him? Indeed, save with a few Americans, such as Mrs. de Trow, who was a firm believer in the divine right of kings, the Legitimist party had little influence left.

As it happened, the vicomte had been in Mrs. de Trow's drawing room on that afternoon when we first introduced her to our readers. Never had the aimlessness of his life as a frequenter of that *salon*, or as a member of society generally, obtruded itself upon him so forcibly ; he was, moreover, irritated at the prominent part played in the conversation by the Sardinian, whom he loathed. On leaving the house, he directed his curricle to the Bois, took a turn around the lake, stopped on the bank, and instead of looking at the throngs of equipages and their well-dressed occupants, actually turned his back on them all, and looked at the swans, the ducks, and the drakes. Then he drove back to Paris, holding his reins very high till his hands almost touched his chin, according to the approved manner of driving among young Frenchmen. Having no engagement for dinner, he dined at a *café*. How a young man passes the evening in Paris will not always bear scrutiny. In the case of the vicomte, he merely went to the theater, repairing afterward to the *Cercle de Jeu.*

While a frequent player, the vicomte had never been a high one. To-night, however, he felt more than usually restless; and, with his craving for excitement, came a strange prophetic instinct that he was going to win. He lost upwards of a thousand louis. He left shortly after midnight, and, as he walked homeward, he reviewed the situation. The impulse that had urged him to play higher than his wont was the pronounced conviction that he was on the eve of great winnings. How odd that he should have lost!

His father's private hotel, in which he himself occupied a bachelor's suite, was situated in one of the streets leading off the quays. It was heavily mortgaged, as was natural, since it had been in the family's possession since Louis the Fifteenth's time. A large gloomy courtyard was in front, and a garden still spacious, but reduced from its pristine dimensions by the encroachments of a new street, lay behind.

The vicomte found his valet awaiting his return stretched out on his best lounge. This did not tend to soothe his irritation; so, consigning the man to the devil, he put on his velvet smoking suit, and lay down on the couch himself. Here he again reflected on the situation. As matters from this new standpoint appeared in no more favorable aspect than from the former, he finally went to bed, resolving never to touch a card again. The ensuing night, he lost ten thousand francs more. The situation was now becoming serious. He could not ask his father to assist him. No, that was impossible. The marquis had all that he could do to raise five hundred thousand francs for a young daughter's *dot*, and her marriage was approaching. The vicomte got up the next morning tired of life and its losses.

Yet it is a long lane that has no turning. He must soon win if he kept up his pluck. Perhaps he had played wildly. Ah! he would adopt a system; then he must infallibly win. He purchased all the literature attainable on gambling—and there is much—and shutting himself up in his apartment for an entire week, he at last selected a principle of play, based on Petti-bone's theory, as the best suited to the occasion.

On the eighth night he returned to the club. As a result of the confidence inspired by his studies he lost twelve thousand francs more.

"*Diable*," he cried, "these systems must have been invented by croupiers. There are but three courses left. I can go to South Africa; I can cut my throat; or I can ask Mme. de Trow to find me an American heiress. Which, I wonder, is the least disagreeable?" But already another alternative was on its way to him.

VI.

MENTION is made of a certain Turkish
ambassador, who, coming to Paris, com·
plained to a colleague of the scant cere·
mony that attended his reception.

"Is your excellency not aware," was the
reply, "that in the eyes of the French
there is nowadays but one ambassador?"

"And who is that one ambassador?"
inquired the Turk in surprise.

"Why the minister of the United
States."

This was in the days when we only had
ministers.

Mr. Jackson was not allowed to remain
long a stranger in Paris. The third day
after his arrival a state carriage, accom·
panied by a troop of cavalry, conveyed
him to the Élysée, where, amid the beat-
ing of drums and the fanfare of trumpets
outside, he presented his credentials to the
President. So favorable had been the

impression left by his predecessor that society, too, stood ready to meet him with open arms, and his figure was soon destined to become as prominent an object in fashionable as in official *salons.* His very dress coat, to which allusion has already been made, created a deserved sensation. It was of the cut worn by statesmen and diplomats of the old school—your Clays—your Adamses—your Guizots. It was buttoned up tightly across the chest, and carried a certain distinction in its high collar and its narrow sleeves. There was a certain formality, too, in our representative's manner when in public—a slightly oratorical way of conversing—which seemed to belong to the attire, and drew people about him when he talked. It was the forgotten dignity of the old school which, like ripe Madeira in many an American cellar, can be found lingering to perfection in America alone—let us claim. In effect, the ambassador made a decided hit.

To her husband's success, Mrs. Jackson contributed. Her manner had a graciousness, the charm of which was enhanced by a little air of primness.

Nor did their success spoil them. On the contrary, because of it, they were the more ready to appreciate the loneliness of others; and, on this score, if on no other, willingly tolerated the advances of Mrs. Asher.

"I stopped to get you to promise to come and dine with me to-morrow," cried that lady one morning, as she ran in upon Mrs. Jackson. "Remember, you have never set foot in my teeny weeny little house."

"I would have done so long before, my dear," replied Mrs. Jackson, "but I cannot accustom myself to these French cabs. The drivers are so uncivil. They crack their whips and tear along so madly when you wish to go slowly, and creep at such a pace when you are in a hurry, that they are quite impossible. We have engaged a private carriage by the month, but the arrangement does not go into effect till next week. So, as there are no street cars here, I fear we shall have to wait."

"Oh, those dear street cars!" fervently ejaculated the visitor. "I used to love them so as a girl; there is a democratic freedom about them that is quite captivating. The only place where woman is recognized at her true worth is in an American street car."

The visitor turned to a pile of visiting cards that lay upon the table. "Oh, but you are getting into the swim," she continued; "what a formidable array of distinguished names!"

"Yes, people have been very kind to us," answered Mrs. Jackson, "and Mr. Pettigrew has been telling us that the custom here is to return their visits the very next day. I fear we have been a little remiss, for we have been taking them by installments. You see I am carrying on my grandchildren's education, and write the two eldest a long letter every day. It takes up so much time."

"Do tell me about those delightful children. How many are there, and what are their names?"

"There are three in all—one boy and

two girls. Thomas Jefferson, named after his papa—Tommy we call him; then there's Mattie after me; and Loo after her poor dead mother. Do you know, it actually seemed a sin to leave them."

"Poor little tots!" sighed Mrs. Asher, and she seemed lost in contemplation over the sad picture of their desertion. At last she looked up, and, in consoling accents, "Why won't you go out with me to-morrow in my carriage?" she observed. "Your own will not be ready till next week, you tell me, and we might return the visits that still remain due during our drive. Then, after leaving me at home, the carriage could bring you and your husband to dinner—that is, if you are disengaged."

"Oh, I never could allow that."

"But my coachman tells me that the horses will die for want of work."

Mrs. Jackson reflected. "I must admit I should very much like to see your house; and, as it happens, most of our dinner engagements are for evenings some time ahead. To be sure, we had a partial engagement later in the evening with Mr. and Mrs. Lovejoy, but——"

"Why not induce them to come with you? Any friends of yours will be welcome."

Again Mrs. Jackson hesitated. "I am sure they would prove very grateful for the invitation," she said. "You see, Mrs. Lovejoy is a distant connection of mine, and her husband has availed himself of the opportunity of Mr. Jackson's appointment to come and establish himself in business here. Naturally, they have made, as yet, few friends."

"And, if I might inquire, what is the nature of his business?"

"He is starting a dental bureau," replied Mrs. Jackson. "He is a young man of decided talent, and with new ideas in his profession. I can see Mr. Pettigrew disapproves of our intimacy," she went on, "but leaving aside any question of kinship, the innate kindliness of people is the first consideration, and occupying a representative position, as we do, it behooves us to make no distinctions."

" And this Mr. Pettigrew, is he a man of the world? I mean, is he worldly? Does he pretend to give advice as to whom you should know and whom you should not know?"

" Mr. Pettigrew is naturally anxious that we should succeed here," said the lady, standing up for the absent gentleman. " Though a trifle prim and Boston-like, he is considerate and kind. The only trouble is, he has not yet got to know us. We desire to see fashionable people so far as it falls within our official duties, but we do not wish to confine ourselves to them alone, and we even feel under special obligation to those Americans who most require a helping hand."

Mrs. Asher looked at the speaker with an odd expression. During her brief acquaintance with Mrs. Jackson, she had learned to feel, despite the kindness of that lady, an undefined fear of her naturalness and directness. However, Mrs. Asher was not a woman of prejudices; and, though dentists affected her unpleasantly, she sent the desired invitations. She moreover wrote a cordial little note to Mr. Pettigrew, begging him to join the party.

That gentleman's curiosity about Mrs. Asher was very keen, and for once he con-gratulated himself that his evening was disengaged.

The dentist turned out to be a young man with a waxy face, artificial looking whiskers, and a mechanical smile that dis-closed teeth of such superlative whiteness and regularity as to convey the suspicion that their value as an advertisement was not lost sight of.

His wife was a pretty, lady-like little woman—fragile and delicate as Dresden china—with a tendency to give piquancy to the conversation by an occasional inter-jection of "Do say!" "Oh, my!" "Dear me!" "Is that so?"—finding recourse at intervals in the lament that she tried to reconcile herself to being in Paris by imag-ining herself in Elmira. Though her hus-band failed to back her up in these linguis-tic efforts, saying little himself and merely smiling in his plate, the dinner passed off successfully. The hostess was at her best,

Mrs. Jackson was not only an intelligent woman, but possessed a kindly flow of good spirits, while her husband talked entertainingly, as he always did.

On the excuse that they had to look after a new baby, the dentist and his wife retired early; Mr. and Mrs. Jackson followed soon after, leaving Mr. Pettigrew alone with the hostess. Notwithstanding the good cheer, a slight dejection had fallen upon that gentleman, and he smoked on gloomily, for Mrs. Asher had insisted on his lighting a cigarette, and, to keep him company, had lighted one herself.

Mrs. Asher had a gift of reading the inner thoughts of her companions. "I fear you are unhappy," she murmured, after a long pause.

Mr. Pettigrew rose and knocked the ashes off his cigarette.

"Possibly I can interpret your feelings," she continued. "Will you tell me if I am right? You regret that our diplomatic service is not like that of other countries —where high place is usually the result of regular promotion,"

"Madam, I have nothing to say against Mr. Jackson's appointment," replied the secretary.

"Of course not," interrupted Mrs. Asher. "But you can't help admitting that, however great may be his natural gifts, your advice and assistance have been prominent factors in the success he has achieved."

"I have done what I could."

"In a properly regulated service you might have been ambassador yourself," Mr. Pettigrew protested.

"You must not underrate your abilities," replied Mrs. Asher. "With your experience in European courts, and knowledge of diplomatic usage, there is no position that you might not aspire to."

Mr. Pettigrew was not proof against this flattery. "You are right in one respect," he said. "I have had a schooling that leads me to aspire, though it may not assist me to attain. But enough of myself. I am trying to persuade Mr. Jackson to lease a house worthy of the great country he represents, and I am going to invite your coöperation. There, for instance, is the hotel of the Marquise de la Vieille Roche—the best house in the Faubourg. It will soon be in the market, if what I hear of her son's losses at play be true."

"And who is the Marquise de la Vieille Roche?"

"Who is the Marquise de la Vieille Roche?" repeated Mr. Pettigrew. "Why, she is one of the best-known leaders of French society. What the Jockey Club does for a man, her *salon* does for a woman; to be merely seen at one of her Thursday evening receptions opens every door in Paris." Thereupon Mr. Pettigrew proceeded to give a detailed history of the family.

At the close of his recital Mrs. Asher, who seemed extremely interested in the subject, inquired into the amount of the vicomte's debts.

"I have heard them put as high as thirty thousand francs," was the reply; "but, if only one-quarter of that sum, it would be the last feather. You see, I was on the point of arranging a meeting between

Mrs. Jackson and the marquise; but now there is no use, as in any event she will scarcely be able to entertain much."

"Ah, how I wish I had someone to make things easy for me," murmured the lady. "Here I have thrust upon me a great fortune, with little, if any, experience of the world, and no one to advise me save my enemies."

"Enemies!" ejaculated Mr. Pettigrew.

"Well, I have no friends. Do you know, Mr. Pettigrew, I had at first an inkling that you were inimical to me?"

Mr. Pettigrew started and turned pale. He glanced about the sumptuous apartment, at the lofty ceiling, the Boucher panels and *dessus-de-portes*, the rich crimson silk hangings. With the air of luxury an agreeable sense of warmth stole over him. A little hope, unreasonable but vivid, started into life in his bosom, and germinated like the seed of a flower in a sandy soil. The innuendo was too pointed to be misunderstood, yet too vague and ambiguous to be acted on at once; on the contrary, he must act cautiously, and after a desultory conversation he made his adieux and departed, turning over what she had said in his mind, as he wended his way to his lofty lodgings.

He had, if not a recognized position in the great world, at least an *entrée* there. With such a woman and such a fortune, might he not command any position he liked. What glory her wealth would bring to the embassy. Mrs. Jackson would instinctively yield her the *pas*—and affairs would then be conducted according to his own views.

For reasons that will appear later on, Mr. Pettigrew desperately needed a wealthy and sympathetic helpmate in his position as secretary, and for considerations that were neither wholly worldly nor belittling to him. On the other hand, his tenure of office under Mr. Jackson was extremely precarious, and might be severed completely at any moment. Is it inexcusable in him if he considered that phase of the matter also? What would happen should he be turned adrift on the world? But could he win her? She was evidently friendless and despite the tale she had told the ambassador, he was a little skeptical about her antecedents. Nevertheless, she was a grand and glorious woman—with no cavalier protector in sight, and she had intimated that his assistance would be welcome. There was no *quid* without a *quo*, and his spirits became buoyant as he realized the possibilities before him.

While Mr. Pettigrew was returning homeward, indulging in his fond dreams, Mrs. Asher was inditing a note to the Vicomte de Dindon, whose address, course of life, and characteristics, down to the last particular, had been wormed out of the unconscious secretary.

VII.

"ALAS! HER BEAUTY PROVED THE HONEY
THAT CAUGHT THE FLY."

THE letter reached the vicomte at a favorable moment—at the very moment when, after figuring up his assets, he found that they would fall far short of his obligations.

The letter was short, but to the point. "Monsieur le Vicomte," it said, "I have heard that you are suffering from a temporary embarrassment of a pecuniary character. If I am correctly informed, and you can find it convenient to call to-morrow at twelve o'clock, at No. 220 Rue Pelletier, I think I can suggest a means by which your obligations may be met." It was signed Diana Asher, and was marked "confidential."

"Diana Asher," he exclaimed. "Ah! that is a little too much;" then bursting into a little laugh, he surveyed himself in the glass.

"Well, one's looks are of some use after

all," he cried, for it was natural that he should place but one construction on the letter. His temperament being elastic, it raised him from extreme depression to decided gayety, causing his financial troubles to lapse into the background.

A fresh conquest was before him, of a kind he most appreciated; namely, of a woman whose name was on the tongue of Paris. His curiosity, too, was piqued. He had first heard of her during the late carnival at Nice, where she had attracted considerable attention by her equipage, and still more by standing on her balcony and throwing down coins to the crowd. Then she had recently moved to Paris, and again created a sensation by her horsemanship in the Bois. She had appeared once or twice at the opera, and she called herself an American. This was all he knew about her. But it was of a kind to make him regard her as an adventuress of a superior order, despite her reputation of fortune.

Dressing himself with unusual care, and placing a white gardenia in his buttonhole, the vicomte repaired at the appointed hour to No. 220 Rue Pelletier. He found himself before a private hotel, whose appearance, though unpretentious, was yet a trifle stately. The courtyard was of a considerable size, and the trees that showed over the roof of the mansion argued in favor of a garden behind.

Admitted within, he was left to await the coming of the hostess in a small room overlooking this garden. The window was closed and the air heavy with the odor of hothouse roses, which, combined with a certain richness of decoration, somehow contradicted the impressions created by the exterior of the house. While he was taking note of the rare bric-a-brac scattered about, being a connoisseur in such things, Mrs. Asher entered. She was attired in a peignoir of a soft, clinging texture, with a profusion of lace in front, and falling away in graceful folds behind her as she moved.

With an air of gallantry, he raised her pink finger nails to his lips. Mrs. Asher had a hand the like of which few women could show—delicate, tapering, and of the smoothness of ivory.

"You were probably surprised at my writing you," she coolly observed, "and more particularly that I should be aware of your predicament. But I am informed that you are in debt to the extent of twenty-five thousand francs. If you are unable to obtain relief from any other source, my banker is prepared to come to your assistance with a loan of that amount."

The businesslike tone in which this proposal was stated, as well as the abruptness of its introduction, proved slightly disillusioning to the visitor.

"You are my guardian angel," he observed, however, trying to maintain his enthusiasm.

"But the guardian angel makes one condition," she smiled.

"Madame has but to name it," replied the impulsive young man.

"Monsieur le Vicomte, I have reason for desiring to study this great Paris world from another than an outsider's standpoint. I require to be launched."

"Ah, but how can I help madame?"

"Perhaps not you, but madame the marquise can."

"My mother?"

"Precisely. The conditions that I exact are that you represent my wishes to the marquise, and that she become my sponsor."

A shower of cold water would scarcely have equaled in its chilling effects this announcement. For once, he found no words at his command.

Mrs. Asher continued. "She receives every Thursday evening. There is no better plan by which I could make a start than by her inviting me to receive with her."

The vicomte's amazement augmented. "And is that your ultimatum?" he inquired.

"It is."

"Then madame must know I can hardly introduce to my mother——" He stammered, actually uncertain in which sphere to place her—whether in the reputable or in that of the *demi-monde.*

She looked at him in her cool, unruffled manner. Never had her beauty seemed more refined and spiritual. It began to tell on him.

"I know what you would say. Monsieur does not like to introduce a stranger into the bosom of his family. He is even shocked at my request. Very well, I will explain. I am a stranger, and I may have but a short time to reside here—not the time to take the ordinary methods of assuming the position I am entitled to. But, of course, monsieur is right to ask for credentials. He shall have them. I am the widow of a distinguished officer in the United States army, and am, moreover, on intimate terms with the American ambassador and his wife. Under ordinary circumstances, I would rely upon them to introduce me; but, having so recently arrived, they have not yet begun to receive, and my *entrée* through them would be necessarily retarded. They will gladly indorse my statements, however, and will guarantee that she who is addressing you has the right to select her world."

"Of course, if madame is intimate at her embassy, that puts an entirely different light on the matter," said the vicomte. "But suppose my mother should still object," he continued; "she is not easily persuaded."

"You need only remind her," returned Mrs. Asher, "of the inconvenience of having a son turned out of his clubs, thereby creating a scandal which might reflect upon the young daughter whose marriage is approaching, and affect her future prospects by the possible rupture of the engagement. I know French people, even lovers, are sensitive about such things. But at all events, you can explain to the marquise that the son becomes a pariah, having no place in the wide world to lay his head, and affording to the hated republicans the opportunity of saying, 'See of what character are the sons of these great supporters of the throne; they fail to pay their debts of honor!' I think, however, it would be unnecessary to enter into these particulars. A simple request for madame to call upon me will be sufficient. I mean, naturally, after your father, the marquis, has satisfied himself at the embassy as to my status. The rest could be left in my hands."

The vicomte departed. He had a keen sense of honor, but he was young and unbusinesslike. He was, moreover, in a terrible predicament—a predicament that he had never appreciated until her words about the hated republicans had brought it home to him. After all it was no gift that he would be accepting, only a loan to be repaid, and if she were received at her embassy, as she claimed, her status was established. The request was a little *bizarre*, that was all. But after Mrs. de Trow anything was possible in her country-women, he reasoned. Then her beauty, ah, her beauty! her beauty was divine —and this proved the honey that caught the fly.

VIII.

Two secretaries and a military and naval
attaché form the complement of the United
States Embassy in Paris.   Mr. Jackson resolved not to be in haste in filling one of the
secretaryships which was vacant, and for the
time being to allow Mr. Pettigrew to remain
in the enjoyment of the other.   In all
governmental departments, however, there
is some one person, who, if undistinguished
by any particular title, does a large proportion of the actual work.   In such an indi-
vidual the embassy here was not lacking.

Clerk, interpreter, messenger, chancellor,
and, in short, general factotum, M. Jules
Antel, though a typical Frenchman, was
better posted on the traditions of the office,
its routine of business, and its usages than
it was reasonable to expect the ambassadors
or secretaries with their comparatively brief
stays to be; nor should his value be depre-
ciated from the fact that attendance at the

door-bell was included in his manifold duties. There is nothing that requires greater tact and a nicer judgment than the selection of the right people to admit into one of our embassies, except it be the getting rid of the rest without offense.

Mr. Jackson was quick to appreciate M. Antel's good points, and wisely made a friend of him from the first. Besides, the old clerk offered a curious psychological study to our representative, who delighted to draw him out.

One afternoon, as Mr. Jackson was walking up and down his office, according to a habit he had, he thus observed: "Yes, Monsieur Antel, as I think I have said before, you ought to take a vacation some time and go to America."

"*Ma foi*, were I not so old I might follow your excellency's advice. Indeed, I made a voyage once to the coast of Normandy; but I say to myself, 'What is the use of going anywhere since all the world comes to Paris?'"

"You might be tempted to remain and try growing up with a new country."

"But I have already grown up, your excellency, to the extent of becoming gray, and I find Paris much to my taste. I must confess, too, if you pardon my presumption, I prefer our boulevards to those vast prairies of yours, and the cascade in the Bois to the rapids of Niagara."

"I fear you have no ambition, Monsieur Antel," said the ambassador unguardedly.

"Pardon, your excellency; I have a very great ambition, an ambition that has outlived many changes of administration here, but which it seems will never be realized."

"And what is that?"

"Your excellency, it is to have some recognized position here: I mean some official designation in this embassy. In times back when it was but a legation I dreamed of becoming chancellor: that is now perhaps too much to aspire to; but, if I could be entitled interpreter, or chief clerk, and have it put on my card, it would amply satisfy me."

"Monsieur Antel, I am glad you have

made a confidant of me. I will try to get the government to recognize you when I go home."

"As it is," went on M. Antel, "I am without that status which every man of right feeling naturally aspires to possess. My duties conflict too. When I am copying out some state paper I am liable to be sent out on a message; or again, when I am translating some important document, ting-a-ling goes the bell, and I must fly to the door. It is mortifying to one's pride, quite frankly, Monsieur l'Ambassadeur."

The ambassador laughed in spite of himself. "I quite agree with you, Monsieur Antel. Every man should know his position. Your only trouble is, you have disclosed talents in so many lines, the government will be reluctant to dispense with your services in any. But stay, who in the world is that?"

Mr. Jackson approached the window, and saw an elderly gentleman in a high mail phaeton stop before the embassy. His hat brim was large and curled upward. He wore a black satin stock and a tight-fitting frock coat, and altogether bore the stamp of the old school.

"Who can he be coming to see, I wonder?" exclaimed Mr. Jackson.

"Ah! your excellency, there resides on the ground floor a lovely little blonde—perchance the ambassador has remarked her. She is fortunate to-day," and M. Antel, restored to good humor, smiled with the air of an ancient *boulevardier*.

A tinkle of the embassy bell soon dispelled an hypothesis so flattering to the blonde; and a moment later the old clerk, in conformity with his manifold duties, ceremoniously ushered the distinguished looking stranger into the apartment.

"Allow me to introduce to your excellency the Marquis de la Vieille Roche," said M. Antel.

The ambassador bowed. "And in what manner can I serve the marquis?" Mr. Jackson asked.

M. Antel consulted for a moment with the visitor, and then, in his character of interpreter, thus began: "Your excellency, the marquis begs to express his great respect for the country that you represent, and to say that since your arrival he has heard nothing but the praises of the new American ambassador.   He bids me, therefore, say that he has great honor in making your excellency's acquaintance."

Again the ambassador bowed.   " Please assure the marquis of my appreciation of his complimentary words," replied the envoy, " and remind him I am anxious to hear to what I owe the honor of his visit."

" Pardon, your excellency, I'm coming to the point: briefly, then, the marquis wishes to learn what you know of the antecedents of this American woman, Mrs. Asher."

The ambassador was slightly annoyed. It seemed an officious inquiry, and Mr. Jackson knew how to resent a liberty.   In these cases he put on an air of stony indifference, for which he was celebrated when in Congress.   He shook his head from side to side. "Tell him, Monsieur Antel, that we have no women in America."

" No women in America?" repeated the clerk in natural surprise.

The ambassador kept on shaking his

head. "No, Monsieur Antel. I've known America for upward of fifty-eight years, and there's not a solitary woman in the land. Tell the marquis we only have *ladies* in America."

"Ah! I see," returned the clerk; "then, your excellency, the marquis has come to learn the antecedents of this lady."

Again the ambassador shook his head. "Tell him, Antel, that we have no antecedents either, in America: that antecedents equally with ancestors are tabooed. Tell him that so long as people with us keep out of debt and the divorce courts, aye, and you might add, out of city politics, they rank with the best, and have only to account to God Almighty and their own conscience for who and what they are. What does he say to that, Monsieur Antel?"

"He says, your excellency, that he has only one son, who is all to him in this world. He says, your excellency, that he fears his son has developed a sudden regard for this Mrs. Asher, since he has begged his mother, the marquise, to call upon her and try to make her stay in Paris agreeable;

that he, the marquis, therefore, desires to learn all he can about the lady, as your excellency must admit is, under the circumstances, both natural and proper."

Mr. Jackson advanced and cordially extended his hand. He was a warm and generous man, if sometimes a touchy one. "Tell him I have got a son myself—Thomas Jefferson—named after the great founder of our liberties, and that I can respect his son's sentiments for the lady. Tell him that her husband was once an officer in the United States army, whose appointment to West Point I myself secured while in Congress. Tell him, Antel, that this was considered sufficient to secure to the widow the protection of the United States Embassy and my own approval of my wife's acquaintance with her. You might add that, while entertaining the highest regard for the rank and position of Mme. the Marquise, I labor under the impression that a lady who is my wife's companion is fit to room with a queen. Has he got anything to say to that?"

"He thanks your excellency," went on

the interpreter, "and begs to say that you have completely satisfied him—that the marquise will consider it an honor to make the lady's acquaintance, as it will afford an equal honor to the marquis himself. He also begs to apologize for the liberty he has taken in making these inquiries, and to assure you of his most distinguished con-sideration."

Thereupon the marquis bowed, and was escorted by M. Antel to the stairs with extreme ceremony.

IX.

SIGNOR DE MARACOVINI AND MR. DE TROW
MAKE A DISCOVERY OF SUPERLATIVE
IMPORTANCE.

IT seems trite to say that the difference between the French and ourselves is that they make a business of their pleasure, while we make a pleasure of our business. The French even go further, and make of living both a science and a fine art. In spite of the pitying condescension which it is the fashion of some nations to display toward them, they are yet the only people who live as if they had a right to hold up their heads and enjoy life, without the in-dividual possession of a million. They are self-sufficient, therefore self-satisfied; gifted with the capacity of taking pleasure in little things, they have happiness within easy reach; and, passing much of their time out of doors, dyspepsia is well-nigh unknown among them. Sitting at little tables before their *cafés*, they watch the passing crowds, drinking in the beauties of their environs along with the orgeat or *eau sucrée*. On the Champs Elysées of a fine afternoon, the throng of spectators is usually immense; and, despite the influence of a republican government, the sight outrivals any city in Europe.

There was an equipage descending the avenue to-day, however, that would have been worthy of the halcyon days of the Empire, for its magnificent high-stepping horses, if for nothing else. Silk stockings and powder were not frequently seen on the streets now; but the subordination of all colors in the appointments to a subdued green rendered these a fitting adjunct to the general richness. Like a shell borne along on the wave of travel, high above the vulgar flotsam of the tide it came. With the C springs curling like the lines of a breaking wave-crest behind her, reclined on the back seat a woman whose delicacy of contour, whose slender figure, and whose exquisitely fitting black clothes gave an air of indescribable distinction to the entire turnout.

Among those who noticed the approach of the vehicle were the secretary of the

Sardinian legation and Mr. de Trow, who happened to be enjoying a couple of little seats near the curbstone, at two sous an hour. The former, springing to his feet, hastily proposed to his companion that they secure a cab and learn the destination of the carriage.

Mr. de Trow consented with the alacrity of one who has a long afternoon of absolute idleness before him, and they were soon in pursuit. Down the broad avenue the carriage goes, and, traversing the Place de la Concorde, takes the bridge, at the foot of which the columns of the Chamber of Deputies stand like a file of giant soldiers on parade. Arrived at the other side of the river, it passes along the quays, and, finally turning down a side street, rolls into the courtyard of the Hôtel de la Vieille Roche.

"You could have knocked me down with a feather," exclaimed Mr. de Trow a couple of hours afterwards, when relating his adventure to his wife.

"I must confess," replied Mrs. de Trow, "the presumption of this woman passes all bounds—to go and call upon a perfect stranger."

"But the marquise called upon her first."

"The marquise called upon her first," repeated Mrs. de Trow; "impossible!"

"But it is true. You see that was the first question that suggested itself to Mara-covini and myself when we saw her drive in. Could she have gone to see the marquise of her own accord, or had she called to return a visit? This we discussed in all its bearings till, in fact, we saw her come out and drive away; then, resolving to ascertain at all hazards, we rang the lodge bell, and, frankly stating our dilemma to the *concierge*, gave him a louis to find out for us. This he did through one of the footmen who had been on the carriage the day the marquise called, and who distinctly remembered leaving her card for Mrs. Asher."

"If Americans are coming to inundate French society like this, there'll soon be little credit in being in it. She can have no position at home; and, if it was not so sad, it would be actually laughable."

For Mr. and Mrs. de Trow assumed to hold the first and only mortgage on the Faubourg. Mr. de Trow looked as if no words could adequately express his sense of personal grievance.

"Yes, it's more than presumptuous— it's monstrous," continued the lady; "and what makes it worse, I suppose we shall soon have to go now and call upon this Mrs. Asher ourselves."

X.

MRS. ASHER CAPTURES THE FAUBOURG.

Mrs. Asher had timed her visit well,
for she found the marquise at home, and,
moreover, made a good impression on her.
Our fair compatriot had an extraordinary
facility in languages, and an equally remarkable gift of adapting herself to all
kinds of people. She told the marquise
that she wished to do good in the world
(Mrs. Asher was always talking about
doing good in the world). She explained
her theories of the obligations of great
wealth. She said, too, that she was a
Roman Catholic, and intimated a desire to
consult the Archbishop of Paris concerning the best field for certain charities.
Further than this, she alluded to the deca-
dence of the higher virtues consequent
upon the spread of democracy, and touched upon the advantage that might even
yet accrue to the Legitimist cause
by the disbursement of sufficient money

in the coming elections. Thus she arrayed, as it were, the Church and State in her favor, and quite took the old lady by storm.

The marquise was a plain, simple-minded woman, whose every effort was required to fill the duties of a great position on a limited income: a woman belonging to an age that was not familiar with the scheming adventuress; and she owed her position to the historic name she bore rather than to any whim of fashion—a woman whose character was not unlike Mrs. Jackson's in its simple dignity.

It is to the credit of French society that these women are looked up to, and are not relegated to the shelves of obscurity, as such dames are apt to be in England. They are the antidotes to the parvenu who is demoralizing society.

An invitation to the marquise's Thursday evening receptions followed; and, a few nights afterward, Mrs. Asher made her first public appearance in the great world of Paris. Her success was immediate and unquestioned. She seemed the very quintessence of refinement, devoting all her efforts to capturing the good-will of the women, and appearing to shrink away from the men, who were thereby only drawn to her the more. For Mrs. Asher knew that it is only when a woman's position is sufficiently assured to enable her to brave the hostility of her own sex, that she can afford to encourage the devoted attentions of the other. Thus, by one bold spring, she had placed her foot on the highest rung of the social ladder; for, if you only have the courage, it is as easy to begin at the top as at the bottom, and you save much intermediate climbing.

Among those most astonished at her *début* was Mr. Pettigrew. He was also dismayed, for he realized that she was now lifted out of his reach, and that his new-found hope would have had a far better chance of realization had she remained obscure. But she was too clever a woman to neglect him. On the contrary, she rather encouraged him, seeming to shrink less from him than from other men.

Nor was the vicomte quite satisfied,

either.   Had she continued under his protection, the admiration of the world would
have flattered his pride; but she had
profited too greatly by his assistance, and
seemed escaping also from him.

A few days after, he called by appointment at her house.

"But you have not given me my reward,"
he said, taking a seat beside her on the
empire sofa.

"And what reward is that?" she asked,
a trifle nervously.

"A little affection."

She could not yet afford to show her
independence. "But affection is not always
at our command," she smiled.

The vicomte endeavored to secure her
hand. "Then you must give me a chance
to woo it."

She avoided his touch, as only a clever
woman can do. "But, Monsieur le Vicomte, you are 'too previous,' as we say in
America. Fie! fie! what would the
maître d'hôtel think if he found us sitting
hand in hand."

"He would probably imagine that we

were playing Paul and Virginia," said the young man sarcastically.

"He would certainly think it very strange. But tell me something about these de Trows; they left cards on me yesterday. Do you know them?"

"I know them," replied the vicomte gloomily.

"Well, what sort of people are they?"

"Mrs. de Trow is an inspired goose," returned the vicomte still sulkily, "who owes her position to her peculiarities."

"Ah, how delightful! You make me anxious to know her. In what does her peculiarity consist?"

"In her efforts to be like other people."

"That is better than trying to be different. It is not a pose, then?"

"Perhaps not; but we are getting off the subject. I told you that from the first moment I saw you, I fell a ready victim to your fascinations. Have you no regard for my affection, that you cast it off like a glove?"

"What is affection," asked Mrs. Asher

drearily. "I knew it, or thought I knew it once, but I was deceived."

"That ought to make you more appreciative of it when it is genuine."

She laughed. "But its genuineness can scarcely be proved in two weeks."

"Do you not believe then, madame, in the spontaneity of affection—in love at first sight?"

"I am more inclined to believe in love *before* first sight."

"In love before first sight," repeated the young man confusedly; "but how so?"

"I fear it would seem coarse if I explained."

"Nothing would seem coarse from your lips."

"Very well, then. When a man desires to *ranger* himself and he hears of a lady with three millions in the Rentes, *his* is apt to be a case of love before first sight."

"Madame is ironical."

"Madame is only practical. Real affection requires more than three or four meetings, my friend, to develop;" but she looked at him encouragingly, all the same.

" How many does it require ? " asked the vicomte doggedly, forgetting that of all things a woman most dislikes being pestered with questions.

"Oh, we will not discuss that now. Here comes another visitor;" for Mr. Pettigrew's card was brought in at this moment. " You know I must tolerate him," she continued in an aside, " he is such a friend of those dear Jacksons."

Mr. Pettigrew was quick to follow his card; and, as he entered, he eyed the vicomte with as near an approach to annoyance as he deemed it politic to bestow on anyone who might ever prove useful to the embassy. The vicomte, after a curt salutation, walked over to the window.

It requires tact of no mean order to keep two gentlemen in good humor who meet in the drawing room of a woman on whom each considers he has an especial claim. Each immediately decides to outstay the other; and this in itself is embarrassing. But Mrs. Asher was equal to the occasion, and gradually brought the two men together by her sprightly talk.   Finally she repaired to the piano; and, having made Mr. Pettigrew comfortable on the sofa, permitted the vicomte to turn over the leaves of her score.

While her voice was lacking in power, it was of remarkable clearness, with a ready flexibility that enabled her to slide without apparent break or inconsistency from the most risky solo of the "Timbale d'Argent" to the "Ave Maria" of Gounod. As she went on, the vicomte began to hum such strains as were familiar to him in a harsh jerky tone, emphasizing the more inspiring parts with one hand as he turned over the score with his other, leaving Mr. Pettigrew occasionally to break in from the sofa with his own voice, which was a trifle thin, or at other times to clap enthusiastically as he cried, " Brava ! brava !"

When she rose from the piano, it was with the excuse of an engagement to drive; and the two gentlemen were obliged to depart together. As he emerged into the street, the vicomte detected the Sardinian secretary watching the door from a cab around the corner. He breathed a silent malediction. Clearly Signor de Maracovini was waiting the withdrawal of the visitors to call himself. "*Sapristi*," muttered the vicomte when he reached the next corner, "the whole diplomatic corps are lying in wait," for here he flushed the Bohemian and the Sicilian ministers earnestly conferring together. Probably they had been speculating as to whom madame had been receiving; for curiosity fills a large part of the modern diplomat's time.

XI.

MRS. DE TROW was nothing, if not patronizing.

"You must let me give you a word of advice, now and then," she observed to Mrs. Asher, when that lady came to return the former's visit. "Paris is divided in the opinion whether I am a fool or a genius; but I see things quite plainly, I can tell you."

"Oh, will you give me your advice?" exclaimed the visitor, in her brightest, most naïve way; "I *shall* appreciate it. You know I have seen *so* little of the world."

"I often think the less one sees of the world, the better," retorted Mrs. de Trow. "One becomes demoralized, my dear, actually demoralized. The men we meet here have but one idea—to take advantage in some way of our sex."

"And what is the predominating *motif* of our own sex?" laughed Mrs. Asher.

"To encourage them."

"I know very little of France and its people except through its literature," observed Mrs. Asher more seriously, "but it has often occurred to me this must give a very false impression of life here. The so-called realism we see in French novels, and in French art generally, can hardly represent more than a mere passing fashion —the natural reaction from the absurdly stilted romantic school that preceded it. The sum total of a people's virtue, you know, must be about the same all over the world."

"Don't deceive yourself," said Mrs. de Trow decisively; "things have arrived at such a pass that for women of any pretensions life becomes one long and continued state of defense. Why, my dear, we are reduced to an actual condition of siege, and the expedients to capture, often only to compromise us, would never be realized except by those who understand the contemptible drift of the masculine mind."

"Ah," exclaimed Mrs. Asher.

"Yes; for, like the Indian with his scalps, a man counts his social status by the number of his conquests over poor us. Indeed, on calmly reviewing the situation," continued Mrs. de Trow, after a plaintive pause "I am almost persuaded to return to America, or to seek refuge in some monastery, far from the world."

"You surprise me very much," returned Mrs. Asher demurely. "But what were you going to advise me—to enter a monastery also?" There was a slight stress on monastery.

"Well, I've quite forgotten. Oh, yes, I was simply reciting my experiences of men to put you on your guard. And yet, and yet," here the thought of Signor de Maracovini recurred to her, "we must not be too hard, only never let them go too far."

"Too far away?" inquired Mrs. Asher innocently.

"Yes, nor too far near you. For, I suppose, we must consider the man's point of view—despicable as his sex is. He needs our influence. There is nothing that brings him out like a grand passion——Take de Trow——"

"I take him!"

"You may," with one of her sudden turns, "I won't be jealous, but I meant to take him *for an example*. How a grand passion would revivify him! Why, it would make him quite a new man."

The idea of a grand passion in any con·nection with Mr. de Trow struck Mrs. Asher as amusing, and she smiled in spite of herself as she rose to go.

"By the way," said Mrs. de Trow, de·taining her visitor, "speaking about Indians and scalps a moment ago reminds me that I am getting up a party next Tuesday evening for this horrid Wild West Show. Its very vulgarity, I believe, has revived interest in it here, and I want to secure your company. You will promise to come, will you not?"

Mrs. Asher cordially accepted the invita·tion.

XII.

WHEN Tuesday evening arrived Signor
de Maracovini apparently still believed in
the Machiavellian policy he had adopted;
consequently it was his attentions, rather
than Mr. de Trow's, of which Mrs. Asher
was the happy recipient. In fact, the Sardinian hung about her the entire evening,
moving his seat next to her as if he considered it his special province to explain
each tableau in the thrilling performance,
and assuming a guardianship over her that
was certainly exasperating to Mr. Pettigrew
and to the vicomte, if it had no particular
effect on Mrs. de Trow, for whose benefit
it was more especially intended.

The vicomte kept twirling the little
points of his mustache, till he looked as
sullen as Othello in the act of working
himself up to the climax of suppressing
Desdemona. And as for Mr. Pettigrew,
that pallor of his parchment-like com-

plexion became more pronounced as he nervously twisted his kid gloves, which in ac-
cordance with a general scheme of economy,
he more frequently kept in his pocket than
wore on his hands.

Among other incidents of the evening
might be mentioned the fact that, owing to
a proclivity of Mrs. de Trow's servants to
take advantage of her every absence, there
was no one to receive the supper she had
ordered from an adjoining restaurant.
Consequently, on her return with her guests
from the circus, she found it waiting on the
landing. The English diplomat broke his
penknife in trying to pick the lock of the
door, and the efforts of the Egyptian minister to effect a circuitous entrance into the
apartment through the air-shaft signally
failed; so Mrs. de Trow ordered the repast
spread on the staircase, thus originating a
style of entertainment which, under the
name of "*soupers à l'escalier*," subsequently
became the rage.

The unconventional manner of service
led the guests to throw off the restraints of
the dining room; and, in the good spirits

that reigned, the devotions of Signor de Maracovini to Mrs. Asher came in for their fair share of banter.

Now Mr. Pettigrew did not attribute any particular meaning to this devotion, yet allusion to it irritated him and increased his own sense of remoteness from the lady. It accentuated the fact that his own chances were rather receding than advancing; and that with the attentions of which she was the recipient from every quarter, the likelihood of her giving favorable ear to any suit of his was diminishing. Two courses were, therefore, presented to him, namely, to speak at once, or to wait till it was too late to speak at all. Amid the restless tossings of a sleepless night, he decided on the former course, and to delay no longer than the morrow.

XIII.

Now, the secret spring of Mr. Pettigrew's every action as we know was pride in his embassy. It remains to be explained what this pride cost him. To be explicit many of those restorations and repairs in connection with the embassy not strictly necessary from the standpoint of Washington were yet essential from his and had consequently been done at his own expense. For instance, the carpeting of the corridors—the repainting of the woodwork—the rebinding of all the official documents.

With so many demands of a public nature on his slender salary, Mr. Pettigrew was yet expected to live up to a certain standard. Consequently recourse had to be had to the most distressing little expedients to make both ends meet. These extended to his very apparel, and his precise and formal manner were actually attributed by his enemies (for Mr. Pettigrew had enemies) to the complicated part played by pins in his underwear. Talk of your heroes willing to die for their country! How many would live for it on short commons? Life to Mr. Pettigrew was one long sacrifice to his ideal, and if a tenderer sentiment had crept into his suit, we must remember that it had been inspired by the patriotic consideration of the luster his acquisition of Mrs. Asher would shed on the embassy, and in consequence on the name of America among the nations.

Now, the toilet of such a man is a matter of no little difficulty, and the excuse for this long digression is that, while in the act of dressing next morning, an argument occurred to Mr. Pettigrew which, if properly urged and emphasized, he thought might better influence his fair compatriot than any plea connected with the embassy. It was none other than the superiority in the way of domesticity of American husbands over those of any other nationality or race.

On the eve of any important step in life,

Mr. Pettigrew strained a point and break-
fasted sumptuously, recognizing that the
extravagance was amply repaid in the
increased confidence with which a generous
meal inspired him. His plan of action
decided upon, he repaired to Voisin's at
twelve o'clock. Oh, the ecstasy of such a
breakfast as he ordered! As it progresses
you feel the good cheer warming the
cockles of your heart, penetrating the
innermost recesses of your diaphragm, and
filling you with a gentle hopefulness that
puts the world at your feet.

A French *chef* once remarked that with
the advent of the republic his divine inspiration had evaporated; that the dull
monotony of democracy, with its principles
of equality, which reduced everything to the
same dead level of commonplace, had first
affected cooking, and, through cooking, was
destined to destroy all the minor arts—
literature, painting, music, and the drama,
—of which his own was the true and god-
like parent. Very likely he was right; but
I think there is something in the very air
of Paris which, despite the form of govern-

ment, appeals to every sense and quickens every appetite.

Mr. Pettigrew, having finished his breakfast, left the restaurant. All the world seemed *couleur de rose* and scented with the fumes of *château la rose.* He took a cab and drove up the Boulevard des Italiens; and, as he went, he forgot that reclining against the cushions tended to make shiny the back of his frock coat. That it deranged the mechanism of his improvised shirt-front to turn his head too far to the right or the left. He forgot that holding his leg so displayed a needle mark in his best trousers; but in his oblivion of all these little economies and regulations of his daily life he was happy. He rehearsed, *sotto voce* the rôle of the ideal American husband till he had it by heart, insisting on the virtues of the type, the domesticity, the subordination of every longing and desire to those of the wife, until he actually lost himself in the part. Ah, what a husband he would make with such a woman and such a fortune! Life would be as smooth as the pavements over which he was now gliding, and as pleasant as the sights about him. Mrs. Asher knew exactly what he had come for before he entered the room. A woman's instinct can tell these things by the very sound of the bell—the knock at the door—the stepfall on the carpet. She received him kindly, nay sympathetically, letting her hand linger in his, and looking into his expressionless eyes with deep meaning.

Mr. Pettigrew rightly imagined himself a man of action—one of those who seize their opportunities. Encouraged by her manner, he deemed it better to come at once to the point than to risk a possible interruption through circumlocution.

"Mrs. Asher," he said, "I have come to talk on a matter that is very near my heart"; and he laid his hand over that organ, regardless of his determination to confine himself to argument alone. "I hope you will not consider me abrupt if I say that ever since that evening when you told me of your friendlessness, I have thought of nothing but you. From that

moment you have occupied my every
thought. I resolved to prove to you that
you could always rely on me: that I would
always be a true friend. Is it surprising
that friendship has at last become too cold
a rôle? My dear Mrs. Asher, I cannot
offer you wealth, or youth, or a great position, but I can offer you the security of a
devoted attachment which may protect
you from the designing schemes of the
people about you" (Mr. Pettigrew could
not resist this little dig at his rivals).
" Mrs. Asher, I think you will admit, after
what you have seen of the world, that we
Americans make better husbands than any
other nationality. Consider our submis-
sion: reflect how we toil that our wives
may shine. Note our domestic habits—
our subordination of every longing and
desire to that of our wives, and then decide
whether a life-long devotion and homage
from one of us is not better than rank,
title, or riches." And a look of anguish,
coming across the suitor's face opportunely,
gave the exact emphasis required for such
an appeal, though it was only caused by

the derangement of a pin in the back of his collar.

In Mrs. Asher's face the expression of sympathy deepened; perhaps she discerned that his pain was real, and pitied him. She put her two hands on his. "My dear friend," she murmured, "you affect me strangely by what you have just said. I am deeply sensible of your worth, and of the prize that you offer me; for I have experienced the devoted attachment of our men, and can appreciate them at their true value as husbands. But I know you will not wish me to decide too quickly. You must give me time—time to consider the inestimable boon you lay before me. In the meanwhile I must be absolutely free. Should I find the inclinations I now feel toward you become less pronounced than they at present seem, you will forgive me, I know, and not consider that I have trifled with your affections. A woman should not be urged to act upon the impulse of the moment."

Mr. Pettigrew departed in a condition not far removed from ecstasy. He had secured so much more than he had expected.   Therefore he could view with equanimity Señor de Maracoviñi, who happened to be entering the house as he left, and could, moreover, feel for the Sardinian a little generous pity.

"She would not act on impulse." This meant that her impulses were, of course, in his direction, and that she regarded as tempting the offer he had made. Her words must mean, that at the present moment, he was beloved.

How such a recognition raises a man in his own esteem! As Mr. Pettigrew walked homeward his head was in the clouds. Who can blame him if his happiness over her avowal were not entirely confined to patriotic considerations?

XIV.

YET it was the vicomte's chances which were considered the best. His curricle drove up and down her street every day, and at the parade of the four-in-hand club Mrs. Asher certainly occupied the box seat by his side, much to the annoyance of Mr. Pettigrew and Signor de Maracovini, who rode on a back seat of the coach just behind.

A circumstance that puzzled the vicomte, captivated the English attaché, caused Sardines to marvel, and troubled Pettigrew, was the acumen she displayed in regard to horses. While neither by garb nor accent suggesting that most disillusioning type of femininity, a horsey woman, she yet evinced an equine knowledge that set every one to wondering where and how she could have acquired it, naming three consecutive winners on the day of the Grand Prix. Signor de Maracovini, however, continued his attentions to her, regardless of the vicomte and Mr. Pettigrew; and while Mrs. de Trow would never have admitted, even to herself, that these attentions could excite in her breast so vulgar a sensation as jealousy, they nevertheless irritated her. Women, more than men, I think, are prone to estimate value according to demand, and only require the object of their regard to seem wavering in his allegiance in order to advance their bids.

Thus one afternoon, when Mrs. de Trow noticed her lover cold and preoccupied, she rashly proposed, as a means of reviving his waning interest, that he take her to dine *téte-à-téte* at one of the restaurants on the Boulevards, naming an evening in the near future which would be agreeable to her. Though Mrs. de Trow was one of those fortunate women who can fly in the face of conventionality without incurring the hostile criticism of the world, she nevertheless rather repented of this suggestion as the time of her appointment approached. Had it not been for her maid, she might have sent an excuse at the last moment.

Mrs. de Trow, of course, did not explain her intentions to her attendant, merely stating that she was to dine *en ville;* but, when she ordered a certain dark toilette laid out together with a black bonnet and a heavy blue veil, Élise divined what was up, and lent such cheerful encouragement that the adventure seemed robbed of any danger. Perhaps Signor de Maracovini had purchased her co-operation.

Now Mrs. de Trow made a point of maintaining an inviolable secrecy from her husband touching her engagements with the other sex. The necessity of this course was a pleasing fiction, since Mr. de Trow had long ago given up the attempt to exercise any control over madame, having yet that absolute confidence in her capacity to take care of herself that reconciled him to his loss of authority.

This evening, however, she herself gave her secret away, as she deemed it prudent to replenish her pocketbook against any unforeseen contingency.

"Wouldn't you like to know where I am going?" she asked lightly, as she put

the hundred-franc bill her spouse gave
her in one of those mysterious receptacles
hidden away between flounce and bustle
where women carry their money.

"Oh, certainly, my dear," said Mr. de
Trow. "I always like to know where you
are going."

"But suppose you should not approve,
then you'd be sorry to learn, and you would
have gained nothing by my indulgence."

"That's true," replied monsieur philo-
sophically. "So perhaps you had better
not confide in me."

The answer irritated the lady.

"I think I *will* tell you though," she returned a trifle recklessly. "I am going to
dine with Signor de Maracovini at Bignon's
tête-à-tête. What do you think of that?"

"Poor fellow!" sighed Mr. de Trow.
"As for me, I am going to have a comfortable dinner at home. But what time is
your engagement for?"

"Eight o'clock."

"Eight o'clock," replied Mr. de Trow,
looking at his watch. "Well, my dear, if
you're really going, I'd advise your starting

soon or you'll be late. It's now gone half past seven."

The idea of setting forth on such an outing under these discouragingly encouraging conditions! The reply was too much for the lady's equanimity.

"Percival, do you know, I think you the most provoking person I ever saw."

"And why am I provoking?" he asked in natural surprise.

"Because there are times when a woman longs for opposition. Far better to be sworn at, reviled, beaten, than to receive this flabby acquiescence that always meets my most startling proposal."

"That's only the pleasing delusion of a woman who has never been subjected to the treatment you describe," interjected Mr. de Trow.

Mrs. de Trow failed to notice the deep philosophy of the remark. "You have no spirit," she continued. "I sometimes feel you will drive me to the divorce courts."

The idea of a woman claiming a divorce from her husband because she was not dragged about the floor by the hair of her head, is one of the most singular evidences of feminine inconsistency that I know of. Poor Mr. de Trow's patience was nearly exhausted, however, and he failed to see the situation in its true absurdity.

"Now look here, Dora," he exclaimed petulantly. "I know what your object is. Simply to increase your own enjoyment this evening by feeling you have destroyed mine."

"I deny it," said Mrs. de Trow. "I wish you to object. I want you to put your foot down and, with a great big round 'd-a-m,' say I shall not go to dine with any man alone."

"But what would be the use? My objections would have no effect."

"Yes they would. They would heighten my satisfaction in going. As it is, you have robbed my entire evening of its spice; but good-night, you'll be sorry some day, Percival; good-night," and at last, appreciating that she really would be late if she lingered longer, she swept her husband's cheek with a forgiving kiss and departed.

She found the Sardinian walking impatiently up and down the stuffy little room on the *entresol* where he had ordered dinner. Red morocco lounges ran around the sides of the apartment. It was low ceiled, and over the backs of the lounges were successions of mirrors.

Mrs. de Trow uttered a little scream as she caught sight of the muffled blackness of her figure reflected in the mirror. Why is it that women, when keeping a clandestine appointment, so frequently indulge in a profusion of lugubrious-hued wrappings? Do they consider them inconspicuous, and so hope to escape observation? So heavy were Mrs. de Trow's, so funereal her general appearance, that a gloom fell upon her admirer as he unwound her. It was as if she had put on mourning in advance for an expected loss of innocence. Though she laughed when the last fold was unwound, her very attire seemed to confirm her previous doubts as to the propriety of her conduct; and, by some feminine instinct, she avoided during the repast any reference to the communion of congenial souls, and absolutely refused to discuss the passions, endeavoring to keep the conversation within the safer limits of her companion's boyhood, the suppression of brigandage in Sardinia, and the effect on Italy of the Pope's last encyclical—of the contents of which, it may be added, she knew absolutely nothing.

Now, for a young man to accept from a pretty woman (and one quite old enough to know beforehand what her condescension means) an invitation to dine at a Paris restaurant, and then to be confined to such inconsequential topics as the Pope's encyclical, is out of all reason, and he has, it seems, just cause of grievance. Every attempt on his part, however, to bring the conversation around to more congenial lines failed. At the introduction of the coffee and *liqueurs*, he had got no further than the general disarmament of Europe, which was the turn she gave to an allusion to the passions—persisting in regarding these from an international standpoint which made their transition to an innocuous condition natural and praiseworthy.

At last, unable to bear the strain longer,

he arose from his seat and angrily surveyed her.

"Why is it, madame, that you keep me at such arm's length?" he said. "When you are in your own house, you talk much about the communion of two spirits that are fitted for each other. You speak about the romance of the soul; but, when there is the opportunity of conversing on these subjects by ourselves and undisturbed, you begin about the politics of Europe. Do you not see that you are driving me to despair? My spirit is always ready, but yours is always in retreat."

Mrs. de Trow sighed.

"Like the coffin of Mahomet, I dangle between the heaven and the earth because of you," the young man went on, "with no expectation of finding a houri in heaven who will cause me to forget."

This was a sad, if indiscreet, admission, and too obviously pointing at Mrs. Asher for Mrs. de Trow to ignore. "Can't you be generous?" he continued. "You lead me like a horse to the water, and when I would drink, you pull away the pond."

Mixed as was the metaphor, there was a world of truth in the protest.

Mrs. de Trow sighed again. "Ah, my poor young friend, you know not what you ask. You forget the grave responsibilities you would be incurring if, if—I allowed myself to return your affection."

"For your sake I am ready to incur any responsibility—for your sake any risks," magnanimously continued the Sardinian. "What is life worth without affection? Love is divine. It raises one to the gods. I have often heard you remark so your-self."

"True."

When a woman under such circum-stances makes use of that little expression "true," a man may as well strike his colors and acknowledge his defeat. It is the thin end of argument's wedge, and has a pain-fully cool, unimpassioned sound. Far bet-ter a yawn. The most encouraging reply is a sigh breathed gently.

"True," murmured Mrs. de Trow, "but the sacrifice would be all on my side."

After "true" invariably comes a "but."

"Ah! now I have your admission," he cried. "It is only about yourself that you care. Why can you not think a little of me? Why can you give up nothing for one who loves——" And, before she could check him, he threw himself upon his knees, and endeavored to draw her hand to his lips. Mrs. de Trow at last appreciated the gravity of the situation.

"Oh, rise, rise, and spare me, young sir!" she cried. "You rend my feelings. See, you make me weep."

Mrs. de Trow was really agitated. That she had suffered such a liberty to be taken with herself wounded her *amour propre*. And yet, her kindly heart was touched. She felt for this warm, impetuous young man. Faintly, too, her conscience reproached her, and she asked herself whether she was not in some slight degree culpable for the encouragement she had given him. Then, hearing the waiter shuffling outside the door—French servants are always discreet, and never enter without some little warning—she took a glass from the table and filling it from a siphon of seltzer, gently presented the cooling draught to her lover. He rose from his knees and angrily dashed it to the floor. Thereupon, Mrs. de Trow herself rose, calmly summoned the attendant, and replacing her wraps about her chaste shoulders, in the most unruffled tone of voice, bade her companion conduct her down to her cab.

Yes, Mr. de Trow was right. His confidence in his wife's ability to take care of herself under any circumstances was well founded.

XV.

How extraordinary are the links of destiny in the chain of human events! It happened that the vicomte dined the very next evening in the same little private room of the same restaurant, and was, moreover, served by the identical attendant who served the Sardinian and his fair friend. The vicomte, however, dined alone, as the companion he expected failed to appear.

French waiters, besides being discreet, are sympathetic—particularly in such cases as these. Desirous of consoling the solitary guest, he gave him, with the exception of Mrs. de Trow's name (which he did not know), the full particulars of her dinner with Signor de Maracovini, and described in picturesque language the prominent part played by the glass of soda water.

Lacking as was the vicomte in humor, there was sufficient in the story to excite his amusement; and, on his return home, he communicated it, for want of a better confidant, to his valet, with whom, in spite of his frequent revilings, he was really on the best of terms.

By a combination of coincidences that would seem unlikely in fiction, but are always happening in real life, the valet had lately been enjoying a little flirtation with Mrs. de Trow's maid, so he communicated the story to her as she did to her mistress. Thus it was brought back to the ears of one of the principal actors in the drama.

Now Mrs. de Trow, though always causing others amusement, was as deficient in any appreciation of humor as was the vicomte himself, or, as for that, as are women generally. She saw but the tragic side of the affair, *i. e.*, the danger of its reaching the ear of the Sardinian ambassador, and affecting the future career of her indiscreet companion—for she knew that there had been a state dinner at his embassy that same evening, and that he had urged illness as an excuse for his absence. She alone was responsible for his breach of official courtesy. Was it not her duty to try and suppress the story before it fairly took wing? She reasoned it all out in her own mind. The Sardinian would certainly resent the vicomte's talking, and there might be a duel. In any event he would, very likely, lose his post. Was it fair to put him in such a situation?

There was a faint flavor of romance about Mrs. de Trow. She did not love the secretary, but she loved to think she did. Indeed, there was very little Mrs. de Trow did love besides sensation. She would send for the vicomte and try to induce him not to repeat the tale. She would throw herself on his mercy in behalf of her friend. There was something exhilarating in the mere thought of the self-sacrifice she was making in confiding her reputation to a man. Before reconsideration could change her purpose, she dispatched a note to the Hôtel de la Vieille Roche urging the vicomte to call at once, upon a matter of the most pressing moment.

Somewhat startled, the young man appeared before an hour had elapsed.

"Madame, you do me great honor by this summons," he said in his jerky way.

"Oh, I pass over your irony," she cried. "I have asked you to come in order that I might throw myself on your generosity."

"Might it not be better to select a chair?" he asked; then, as she took a seat, "and now, madame, will you not have the kindness to specify your reasons for sending for me;" for the vicomte hated being called out before twelve o'clock and he, moreover, began to suspect that the importance of the summons had been exaggerated.

"It is to ask you to refrain from making any further allusions to—to Mr. de Maracovini's dining the night before last at Bignon's."

"And why so?"

Mrs. de Trow blushed. "Because he ought to have dined at his embassy, and, if the cause of his absence leaks out, it might injure his career."

"Signor de Maracovini is fortunate in having such a champion; but, except for your interest, I hardly see what his career is to me, madame."

Mrs. de Trow, perceiving that her visitor was obdurate, resolved upon a grand and heroic course. She rose and drew herself up to her full height.

"Monsieur le Vicomte, if you go on re-peating this story, it may compromise me. You are a gentleman, and I can trust to your honor."

"Madame, no man can ever compromise you."

"It would be discovered that we were dining together," said Mrs. de Trow trag-ically.

"Never mind, madame, you could dine with a regiment without anyone ever suspecting you of wrong." (A regi-ment was a favorite expression of the vicomte's.)

"And why so, sir?" inquired the lady, a little tartly.

"Because madame possesses a greater purity than the driven snow."

"Greater than the driven snow——?"

"Precisely, for snow sometimes melts."

"But what will the world say?   It will not be so lenient."

"It will say exactly what I have said."

Somehow the reply irritated Mrs. de Trow, but she turned it off.

"You believe, then, that I am incapable of experiencing a grand passion.   You believe that I am cold, heartless, cruel, perfidious, or "—and Mrs. de Trow expressed in her eyes as near an approach to resentment as the generosity of her soul would permit—"do you mean to insinuate that I am incapable of inspiring a grand passion?"

"Madame, with you there is nothing impossible—not even that."

"Then let me beg of you to keep this story to yourself," she went on volubly. "Oh, sir, have you never known what it is to love?   Have you never experienced the communion of two souls that are fitted one to the other?"

"Common report has told me much about it," replied the young man meaningly.

"Then promise you will not disturb this sweet communion of ours; promise me that you will be magnanimous, for you must remember, in injuring this poor boy you injure me; and in striking him you strike through a woman's breast;" and Mme. de Trow, carried away by the situation, placed her hands upon her generously proportioned bosom.

"Madame, I will not repeat the story; my silence will be but a small return for the best little comedy I have witnessed in many a day. Madame has missed her vocation. The boards of the Palais Royal are alone the proper field for such histrionic talents."

The vicomte withdrew, leaving Mrs. de Trow mistress of the field. She had gained her point, as she generally did, and the story went no further; but the vicomte's manner, as much as his words, rankled.

Though not a vindictive woman, she was, as we shall see, capable of repaying any little slight; and the vicomte was destined to repent in sackcloth and ashes his injury to this woman's pride.

XVI.

AMONG all the balls which enlivened the
season, that of the Princess de Xamarinda
had been the most eagerly anticipated. It
was given in honor of royalty.

That Mrs. Asher was included as a
guest followed as a natural consequence
upon her chaperonage by the marquise. It
was to insure the acceptance of Mrs. Jackson that she stopped one morning to see
that lady, and was sufficiently fortunate to
find his excellency instead.

"Of course you are both going to this
ball," she said.

"I hadn't thought much about it," replied the ambassador, "but I suppose we
shall drop in for a few moments."

"I'm so glad. Perhaps you will let me
go in with you if I meet Mrs. Jackson in
the dressing room. I do so hate entering

these crowded ball-rooms alone," she continued. "It seems so bold and brazen."

"Certainly, my dear; I can quite understand your feelings. Mrs. Jackson will be very happy to chaperon you."

"Thanks so much. I am also going to ask you another favor. You promise beforehand not to be offended?" and she looked up at him in her confiding way.

"And what is that?"

"Why, that you get a new dress coat. You are not angry that I take a pride in your appearance?"

Mr. Jackson hardly knew whether to be annoyed or not; but there was so much of the bright spontaneity of the child about this woman that he could hardly treat her otherwise than as a child.

"Why, my dear," he said, "I have worn that coat during a large part of my public career, and what is appropriate for the White House——"

"Tut—tut—tut—I once went to the White House and saw a man there without any coat at all. When you are in Rome you must do as the Romans do. They wear coats here, and they wear smart coats."

"I have heard of smart men and I have heard of smart women, but I must confess I never heard of a smart coat."

"Well, I mean one of a later cut—one that will show you off to the best advantage.   I grant you your present coat carries with it a certain air of distinction, but it is that of a bygone epoch, and makes you look far older than you have a right to look.   I fear that you are angry and think I am presumptuous in speaking as I have, but you know I am a privileged character."

"If you are of the opinion, my dear," the ambassador gravely replied, "that my personal appearance would be improved, and that so the interests of the country I represent might be furthered, I will consider what you say."

That evening Mr. Jackson thus addressed his wife: "I have been thinking, Martha, over what you said just before our leaving Dianapolis about my dress coat. Perhaps it does look somewhat antiquated, and it may be that you were right in urging that, as the dignity of the country was concerned, I should order a new one."

"Oh, never mind the coat, Samuel. I have come to recognize that the country has a truer and a more real dignity represented by you in that coat than in one made by the most fashionable tailor. Remember, too, you wore that coat at our silver wedding, Samuel."

"That's true, Martha; but I've noticed that it looks different from those worn by others, and it does not do to be exceptional. The coat answered very well for Washington, where they are less conventional in dress than here, or, I should say, where they make more allowances for one; but I must confess, when I caught sight of myself in a mirror at the Élyseé the other evening, I was forcibly reminded of the suggestive expression, 'a back number.' I think, all things considered, I shall have to order a new one."

XVII.

THE BALL OF A PRINCESS AND WHAT HAPPENED.

THE hotel of the princess was one of the few where the different cliques that constituted the great world of Paris met as on common ground. Republican senators and ex-Imperialists, representatives of the *haute noblesse* and the *haute finance*, members of the Institute, too, and lesser lights of the republic of letters, all sank their differences and were reduced to an amiable fraternity of sentiment under the dual influences of a charming hostess and the best of cooks.

On the evening of the ball the mansion resembled a scene from the Arabian Nights. Electric lights illuminated the fountain in the courtyard, and the winter garden and terraces were hung with Chinese lanterns. Halberdiers in mediæval costume lined the hall, stamping the butts of their spears on the floor in honor of the arriving guests.

It was Lord Dufferin who claimed that America has conquered European prejudice through her daughters. At a rough calculation, the wives of one-quarter of the guests here to-night—and they included some of the greatest names of Europe— were born on our side of the Atlantic. Here was the Duchess de R., one of Michigan's fairest flowers; here the Countess de B., from the Pacific slope; here the Marquise de C., a veritable prairie belle, all filling their new rôles with a grace that was the envy of their sisters born in the purple. Here, too, was the beautiful Lady Summerset de Vere, with her little spouse trotting admiringly behind her; and here was Mrs. O'Hagan of Hoshkosh, mother of the hostess—a determined looking woman of sixty, with many diamonds and much rouge. Here, too, were Mr. and Mrs. Jackson, the former in all the glory of a new dress coat, and the latter in a black moire antique, cut square. Besides these, there were Mrs. and Mr. de Trow—the former bursting from her corsage like a full-blown rose from its petals, and the latter with the

order of the Cincinnati pinned to his narrow chest. Here also was Mr. Pettigrew, vainly dreaming, poor man, of enroll-
ing Mrs. Asher in the embassy; and here,
throwing all others into shadow, was
Mrs. Asher herself, with a circle of diamonds flashing amid the golden tresses
of her hair.

But the ball was principally noteworthy from the extraordinary rumor which
would seem to have originated here to-
night. Before anyone was aware who
started it, everyone was discussing it and
carrying it on. It was to the effect that
the recent appearance of Mrs. Asher in
the great world was not unconnected
with the liquidation of certain gambling
debts of the Vicomte de Dindon. Possibly the ready credence given to the story
by the women was due to the great sensation she had created this evening. Royalty was paying her marked attention, and
this stimulated their zeal in circulating the
rumor; for, though women have much of
the heroic in their nature, and can bear far
more than men in certain ways, the devo-

tion of royalty to one of their own sex is beyond their equable endurance.

How Mrs. Asher learned what was being said of her will never be revealed, but the instinct of some women approaches in its keenness a sixth sense. After supper she made the vicomte a little sign to come to her. Taking his arm, she led him out to the lantern-hung garden where, between the snatches of music that came faintly to them from the ball-room, she communicated to him the remarks that were being made about them both; for he was one of the few who had, as yet, heard nothing.

"I thought I was dealing with a man of honor," she concluded.

"Do you mean to suspect me of having said anything?" he asked in natural resentment.

"I shall have to hold you responsible till you discover the author of these tales," she replied coldly, and then she bade him conduct her back to the house.

"I wish we could go home to Dianapolis, Samuel," exclaimed Mrs. Jackson to her husband, as they were returning from the ball.

"And why so, mother?"

"Oh, I hardly know. I sometimes feel that we don't fit in here; that, in spite of all the attention we have received, we are like people whom despotic governments used to send out of their own country— exiles, as it were."

"I imagine that ninety-nine per cent. of our people at home would willingly change places with us in our exile."

"That may be, but sometimes I go further and ask myself whether it is right that we should remain."

"And why should it not be right?"

"It is difficult to explain, Samuel. I don't wish to set myself up on a pedestal, or to assume a monopoly of all the virtues, but do you know, it sometimes seems to me," said the lady impressively, "that Paris is an immoral city. At least people don't have the same way of looking at things here as at Dianapolis. Perhaps I would be considered old-fashioned, but it always shocks me to see, for instance, married women dancing with other women's husbands and usurping the province of young girls. Paris is more of a world than a city—such a great cruel world too! I think people preserve their individuality more distinctly and are more to each other in smaller places."

"Yes, that has often occurred to me also," replied the ambassador. "Crowds destroy friendship as well as true domesticity."

"But we, at any rate, will always be all to each other, will we not, Samuel? You will never let these crowds draw us asunder, or anyone come between us?"

Mr. Jackson put his arm affectionately about his wife's waist: "I'm not the kind, Martha, to let anyone come between us, am I?"

"But, Mrs. Asher, Samuel, it does seem sometimes as if you took a heap of interest in her."

"Mrs. Asher, why she's a countrywoman of ours. I'm here to protect her. A mere chit of a woman, scarcely more than a child!"

"True, Samuel; but do you know it sometimes seems to me as if she was quite capable of protecting herself."

There was no little shrewdness in this quiet, simple personage.

XVIII.

MRS. DE TROW SEEKS THE PROTECTION OF HER AMBASSADOR.

THE Sardinian continued his devotions to Mrs. de Trow; for, though he keenly resented her perfidious treatment of him, he realized that an open rupture would be a too evident admission of failure. But he was sadly quelled in spirit, and the impulsive manner that had erewhile distinguished him was replaced by a marked listlessness towards the whole female sex.

A few mornings after the ball he was sitting with his fair tamer, submissively discussing, if not European politics, yet matters as little to his liking, when her husband entered. His manner was so disturbed that the visitor found a pretext to retire.

Left alone with his wife, Mr. de Trow flung himself upon the divan, nor were all her questions able to extort from him anything but groans and sighs. At last, gradually regaining his composure, he informed her that, in coming out of his club, royalty had passed him by without recognition.

Mrs. de Trow held up her hands in unfeigned dismay. "O Percival! O Percival!" she exclaimed, "what have you done?" and the delusive dream of being taken up by royalty was abruptly dispelled by a nightmare of social ostracism. For Mrs. de Trow invariably jumped from one extreme to another.

"That's just the worst of it," replied Mr. de Trow. "I did not do anything. It is the result of these confounded reports concerning Mrs. Asher."

Mrs. de Trow's heart suddenly ceased its pulsations. "Why, what do you mean?" she asked. "I don't see how you could have got yourself mixed up with Mrs. Asher."

"Why, simply, the story has got about that we, *we*, originated them, and I suppose royalty cut me to mark his disapproval."

"How did the story get about that *we* originated them?" asked Mrs. de Trow with affected coolness.

"Through the pusillanimity of French society. You see, as soon as Dindon heard of the remarks that were connecting him with this woman, he vowed he would discover their source ; and he has been to no end of people who attended the ball and cross-examined them. On comparing notes, they profess to trace them back to you. Of course, I know it's false, but they consider us foreigners the safest scape-goats ; and, unless immediate steps are taken, I shouldn't be surprised if the hot-headed young fool would be taking me to task for them."

Mrs. de Trow's conscience reproached her. She knew more of the origin of this story than she dared to admit; but to be found out as the author, and to suffer with the discovery any loss of social prestige, was more than she had bargained for. She must endeavor to undo what she had been at so much pains to do. The vicomte was cleverer than she had given him credit for being; he had turned the tables upon herself.

Mrs. de Trow, for all her whims, was a

quick-witted woman. "Percival," she exclaimed hurriedly, "we must go to the
American ambassador."

"But why to the American ambassador?" demanded her husband in surprise.

"Because he will be the proper person to
take up our cause. It has assumed the
importance of an international question.
We must get him to intercede with royalty
in our behalf, or we are lost."

XIX.

NEVER had the rush at the American
Embassy been equal to what it was to-day.
Never had a greater number of perplexing
questions come up at once for solution before any ambassador. Proceedings opened
with a call from an agent of a metropolitan
opera house in a large Western city, who
desired Mr. Jackson's advice in the engagement of a Parisian ballet-corps.

Then came a woman in a state of great
mental disturbance. She hurriedly described herself as the American wife of a
Belgian consul, who, resenting the stand
her mother had taken in certain domestic
difficulties, was endeavoring to secure the
latter's incarceration in a *maison de santé.*

"Oh, sir, you will not let her be shut up,
will you? You will take our side, will you
not? I know the case is a somewhat complicated one. Though serving the Belgian
government my husband was an Austrian

by birth. We were married in Hungary. I was born in Rhode Island, and the circumstances on which he bases his claims as to her insanity having occurred in Valparaiso, the laws of that government may have to be considered."

Mr. Jackson showed the bewilderment anyone might experience at this hysterical enumeration of international perplexities.

Then there was a visitor who desired the United States government to compel a picture dealer to refund the purchase money for a fictitiously signed canvas; and still another, who asked assistance in placing an ice-cream making machine on the Paris market.

These several calls illustrate the diversified requirements and responsibilities of our representatives abroad. Thoroughly worn out, Mr. Jackson at last retreated to the innermost sanctuary of the legation, and sought repose on a sofa; while M. Antel, encouraged by a break in the stream of visitors, settled himself down comfortably at his desk with an old edition of the *Petit Journal pour Rire.* He became deeply engrossed in the account of a dispute before the Odéon Theatre between a little grisette and a man watering the street, who, it seemed, by a careless turn of his hose had plentifully besprinkled a new spring toilette. The incident was trivial (except to the sufferer), but it was written in the sprightly style peculiar to the Parisian reporter. M. Antel had arrived at the climax of the story when the bell on the landing began to ring again, and Mr. and Mrs. de Trow appeared.

"Say I can see no more visitors to-day," cried the much requested ambassador when M. Antel announced their names to his excellency.

Mrs. de Trow followed her messenger to the last barrier. "Oh, sir," she cried, "I am a countrywoman of yours, and I must see you on the most pressing business."

"But madam," protested Mr. Jackson, "I am quite exhausted, I assure you. The secretary, Mr. Pettigrew, will be here in the course of an hour or so. Might I not suggest the advisability of your coming back a little later?"

"But I don't want to see Mr. Pettigrew; I want to see you, sir, and to get your advice on the most urgent question."

"It in no wise concerns a lunatic asylum, does it?" asked our representative cautiously.

"No, sir, not yet; but it may result in that if you will not hear me. Do, pray, therefore, emerge, sir, and cease bandying words."

"Very well, then, madam, I suppose you will wait till I resume my coat," groaned the judge.

A moment afterward Mr. Jackson "emerged" from his retreat. "Oh, sir, what I have to say," cried the lady volubly, "may not seem serious to you. When I come to explain, it may even strike you as trivial, but it is everything to us, sir. How can I begin?"

"Begin at the end, madam; that will make it clear from the first," replied Mr. Jackson epigrammatically; and, thus encouraged, Mrs. de Trow gave an outline of her trying situation, yet artfully laying emphasis on the fact of Mrs. Asher's good name being concerned.

"Do you not see, sir, that the very fact of our being credited with originating these stories gives to them a fictitious value? Mrs. Asher is a compatriot of ours. We are supposed to know that such a thing would be impossible for her. Indeed, if only for her sake, I implore you to go and see the Prince. A word from him will shut the mouth of this impetuous young man, who cannot see that the more he tries to find the author of the story the more he drags Mrs. Asher before the public."

"But I hardly know whether such a mission would fall within my representative duties," said Mr. Jackson doubtfully.

"Nonsense, you are here to protect your fellow countrymen—I mean your country-women. While it would be considered a shocking breach of etiquette for my husband to go and ask royalty anything, it would be quite natural for you, backed up as you are by the authority of the United States. You will, therefore, go and call upon the Prince, will you not, and tell him

our dilemma? Tell him, in fact, that de
Trow is on the edge of despair, and that I
am quite over it."

"Over your despair?" asked Mr. Jackson confusedly.

"No, sir; over the edge of it. But pray
cease capping my remarks. I have no
aptitude for repartee. Now, until you
promise to go, do you know what I will
do? I will take a seat here, and never stir
from your apartment."

"I promise, madam, I promise. I would
see a hundred princes for your sake," said
the judge emphatically. And Mrs. de
Trow, having no further call to remain,
gracefully retired with her spouse.

Now, Judge Jackson was a man who,
when he once gave his word, carried it out
to the letter; and, moreover, without delay.
Though he hardly approved of the under-
taking, yet the fact of Mrs. Asher's being
involved outweighed his objections and he
set off forthwith.

There is no doubt that the successful
American politician has a natural bent for
diplomacy. The mission was decidedly

out of the ordinary for Mr. Jackson, but he was gifted with a tact—a lightness of touch, let us say, which enabled him to treat the most delicate matter successfully. He was championing a woman—not Mrs. de Trow—but a young and unprotected woman; and the result of his visit was that he left the matter in a shape in which he was convinced it was best that it should be left—that is to say, in the hands of a prince whose tact was as great as his own.

That evening he was a guest in the opera box of the President; and, Mrs. Asher being in the house, he found occasion to whisper to her that he had done her a service. A warm pressure of the hand was her only reply. How long the recollection of it lingered in his memory!

How long, too, the recollection of his pressure remained in her memory! Mrs. Asher was on the eve of a crisis.

XX.

A TERRIFYING ORDEAL FOR AN UNATTACHED LADY.

"LIGHT — light — give me more light! Turn on every burner to the full!" and Mrs. Asher flings her fur-lined opera cloak from her fair shoulders, as she is admitted into the hall of her hotel. Something unusual has happened, and her agitation electrifies the sleepy footmen, who have been awaiting her return. Hurriedly they obey her mandate; and, under their rapid manipulation, slumbering chandeliers and candelabra burst into sudden life. Not only in the halls and corridors of the lower floor, but, mounting the stairs, the illumination extends to the drawing rooms, and from them to the whole house.

There is something sinister in this sudden demand for light at one o'clock in the morning. It was as if she would make sure that some shadowy terror, which had followed her in the blackness, should find no congenial asylum here.

Mrs. Asher mounted to the drawing rooms; and, sending for her maid, gave her own personal attention to the lighting of all the burners. This was accomplished by the time her attendant reached her; whereupon, sending one of the footmen in quest of her lawyer, and bidding the rest to retire within call, she turned to her maid. "I have seen him," she cried.

"Where, madame; where?" inquired the woman.

"At the exit of the opera."

"Are you sure?"

"Can you ask me whether I am sure?"

"But how could he have learned that you were here?"

Mrs. Asher flung herself upon a sofa, and burst into a wild paroxysm of tears.

"How did he learn that I was here?" she repeated. "How do I know? I suppose through the press, but it is enough that he is here," and she rocked herself backward and forward in great perturbation. "Rachel," she suddenly observed, with an air of prediction, "remember what

I tell you to-night—that man will succeed in his object yet."

" Why not hand him over to the police then ? "

" And face all the scandal ? No, I would rather die than lose the position I have made with so much difficulty."

" Then, at least for the present, will madame not go up to her room ? "

" No, I have sent for Mr. Charterain. I will await him here."

Mrs. Asher seemed actually to have aged by ten years since we last saw her, so noticeable were the lines in her beautiful face. Her breast rose and fell convulsively, and every now and then she pressed her handkerchief to her lips. For at least an hour she waited before the lawyer appeared. He had made all the haste possible, but he was in bed when the summons reached him, and a considerable distance separated his residence from her own. He was a large, healthy looking man, with a broad, smooth face, and a wonderfully soothing manner. Half French, half American, he was well fitted by ancestry

and training to attend to the international
interests that were confided to his charge
by the large American colony residing in
Paris.

The lady sprang to meet him. "My
worst fears are realized," she exclaimed.
"He has pursued me across the Atlantic.
What am I to do?"

"First explain to me the reasons you
have for believing this."

"I saw him," and the lady shuddered.

"Beyond the question of a doubt?"

"His face was at my carriage window."

"Did he see you?"

"I do not know."

"And you refuse to call upon the authorities for protection should he molest you?"

"I have told you before that I fear the
publicity of doing so. There are circumstances in my past that might come out,
Besides he has still rights, you have frequently told me."

"Then why not act at once on the plan
we have so long had in contemplation?
His reappearance gives it especial value
now."

"You mean——"

The gentleman bowed.

"But after I succeeded, would I not be equally subject to persecution?"

"Not to the same degree. Once free, you regard him from an outside standpoint; and, if he annoys you, you simply hand him over to the first policeman as an ordinary disturber."

The lady sighed. "I fear it is the only course. I will start without delay."

XXI.

**MRS. ASHER'S MYSTERIOUS DEPARTURE AND
THE ODD VISITOR TO THE EMBASSY.**

THE influence of royalty is subtle. A
word here, a word there, a friendly smile
in public, an appreciative grasp of the
hand—these, coming from such a source,
have more effect on society in regard to the
persons they concern than leaders and
editorials in the most widely circulated
organs of opinion.

In Mrs. de Trow's case, the cloud which
seemed descending upon her dissolved;
society ceased talking, nor did the vicomte
care to carry the matter further when
royalty was reported as observing that disputes in any wise connected with a woman's
name were in eminently bad form. Thus
the scandal was nipped in the bud for the
time. Therefore Mrs. Asher, whom these
reports concerned, shared in the benefit of
their suppression. Consequently the astonishment of the vicomte may be imagined
when, on calling the next day at her house,

he found that she had left Paris as abruptly as she had come.

The mail brought a letter quite unsatisfactory in its tone, since it gave no other indication of her plans than that she had been recommended by her physician to a sanitarium for a few months.

Mrs. Jackson, the marquise, Mrs. de Trow, and her other friends received letters little more explicit.

It is needless to say her departure caused a ripple of excitement, even in Paris. Mrs. de Trow regarded this retreat as a rout; and, though she bore the lady no ill-will, she congratulated herself on the slap she had given the vicomte. Yet, as his animosity might be rekindled by the departure, and as it would be well to strengthen the bond of sympathy her troubles had established with royalty, she decided to repair to London, where the Prince now was, and to enjoy as much of the season as remained.

But these are the insignificant consequences of Mrs. Asher's withdrawal. It marks an epoch in this story, and with it a cloud, no bigger than a man's hand, begins to rise athwart the horizon. Mr. Pettigrew read in her departure a confirmation of the suspicion that had been lately forcing itself upon his mind, viz., that his fair compatriot cared little for him, and had simply been using him for her own ends; therefore, with her disappearance, his dream of playing the rôle of ideal husband vanished.

The effect on the vicomte of his desertion by her was, however, more serious. He had a temperament, the peculiarity of which was that he never appreciated anything till he lost it, and then he placed upon it an exaggerated value. For three whole days he shut himself up in his apartments, if not to weep and to wail, at least to gnash his teeth, and to show a stern resolution not to be comforted. On the fourth day he emerged. Taking his curricle, he drove to the Bois and looked, according to his habit, at the ducks and the drakes. Again they gave him an inspiration. It was to consult the police. He did so, and after three weeks' patient waiting, was rewarded by the information that Mrs. Asher had repaired to no sanitarium, but in reality had gone to Kamtschatka in search of a particular herb for the complexion.

The effect on our ambassador alone remains to be recorded. In his heart, too, Mrs. Asher left a void; but being a practical man, he proceeded to replace her image by hard work. To be sure, his predecessor had left little for him to accomplish of a noteworthy character; but, in retaliation for a late tariff bill raising the duty on French wines, the French government had raised the tariff on American wheat. Mr. Jackson laid out, as a worthy object of his ambition, the removal of the tariff on his own country's products without any abatement of that on the French. But the French wine growers, who wielded influence both inside and outside of the Chambers, took a different view of the matter. Loudly declaring that American wheat should not be relieved without a corresponding decrease as regarded their own wares, they had thus far neutralized all his efforts. Mr. Jackson was not easily discouraged, however. Again and again he endeavored to show the narrowness of the wine growers' arguments, spurred on by the dread lest the Chambers might soon adjourn; for his knowledge of parliamentary procedure assured him of the increasing difficulty of getting any business settled in the rush of a closing session. His efforts required frequent visits to the Quai d'Orsay, where the official residence of the minister of foreign affairs is located, and necessitated his own and Mr. Pettigrew's frequent absences from the embassy. On such occasions, M. Antel was left alone to hold the fort, so to speak.

Now, there was nothing that tickled the honest clerk's pride more than being left in sole charge of the United States Embassy. Not that he grew presumptuous, or assumed any disagreeable hauteur before the lesser employees of the establishment; on the contrary, his manner to these became marked by an extra courtliness, from which was studiously eliminated any mortifying reminders of the vast gulf that separated them.

Nevertheless, his admiration for the judge was so sincere that, in that gentleman's absence, he could not resist the unconscious repetition of some of Mr. Jackson's tricks of manner—walking up and down the room with his hands beneath the skirts of his coat, throwing back his head, and, by way of heightening the illusion, occasionally transferring his seat for a moment from his own desk to that of his superior.

It was a pleasant afternoon about a month or so subsequent to Mrs. Asher's departure, that M. Antel was thus reveling in his brief authority, when he was recalled to a sense of the complicated nature of his avocations by the sound of the bell outside on the landing. With a very justifiable feeling of irritation, he got up, crossed the corridor, and, on opening the front door, started back in dismay. For of all the weird-looking people that were accustomed to drop in at the embassy, certainly the one before him was the most peculiar. As M. Antel afterward described him to his friend, the advocate next door, he seemed as tall as the Vendôme column, with a bend in the back, as when

that monument was just beginning to yield
to the ropes of the Communards. A long
beard, streaked with gray, hung to the chin
of the man, the cheeks were white and
chalky, while great eyes, that flashed and
sparkled like a couple of living coals, looked
out from under a stern and yet intellectual
brow. A soft felt hat with a wide brim
ornamented the stranger's head. There
was a semi-clerical cut about his shabby
black clothes, that were yet of a different
stamp from that of any clerical clothes
M. Antel had ever seen. Contrary to what
one might infer from his eye, the manner
of the man was dazed and uncertain; but
what most astonished the clerk was the
fact that he came to inquire how soon Mrs.
Asher was expected back in Paris. Many
people came to inquire about Mrs. Asher,
but they were all of so opposite a type from
this one that, merely replying that the
embassy had no knowledge of the lady's
whereabouts, M. Antel suffered the stranger to wander away, without attempting
to secure any information either about
himself or the reason for his inquiries.

XXII

MR. JACKSON ATTACKED BY THE PRESS BECAUSE OF A WOMAN.

THIS visit occurred about four o'clock in the afternoon; and it happened that neither Judge Jackson nor Mr. Pettigrew reappeared at the office that day. Now, great as was his reliance in Mr. Pettigrew, the clerk preferred to mention the circumstances of the visit to the ambassador first; but, the following morning, being sent out on some message by the secretary, who arrived at the office before his chief, he was absent when Mr. Jackson arrived. On his return, M. Antel found Mr. Jackson engrossed with his mail.

How true it is that the greatest events hinge on trifles, and that trifling things unhinge the most practical minds. In the package of newspaper excerpts, regularly forwarded to him from America, Judge Jackson discovered a long clipping, purporting to be a letter from Paris, and headed by the large and startling query —"Is he innocent?"

The letter gave an exaggerated and an entirely erroneous account of his own visit to royalty; which, according to the writer, was undertaken because of a woman of doubtful reputation, in whose behalf the representative had shown a culpable interest. Then followed a fictitious history of his intimacy with this woman, of his social assistance to her, and of his infatuation for her; Mrs. Asher, though not mentioned by name, being of course, referred to.

Throughout his long and successful public career, Mr. Jackson had been singularly free from hostile criticisms, and particularly from this sort of attack; consequently, he was correspondingly troubled by it. It was extremely unfortunate, too, that the letter came to his notice just when it did, as it caused him to give little heed to M. Antel's account of the stranger who had called the preceding afternoon. It also put him out of temper with his work that morning, and further made him late at the Quai d'Orsay, whither his duties again called him.

In fact he found that the German ambassador had anticipated him, and was now closeted with the minister of foreign affairs. As the interview promised to last some little time Mr. Jackson decided to wait its conclusion in the garden below. Here amid the orange and lemon trees he was walking up and down when his reflections were disturbed by the presence of someone at his side, who was bowing to him in the most polite and formal manner. Mr. Jackson recognized the Vicomte de Dindon, with whom he had enjoyed a passing acquaintance.

"Ah! my young friend, how do you do, how do you do?" said the judge.

"Devilish badly, your excellency," returned the vicomte.

"Well, I'm sorry for that," replied our representative, "but if it will console you, I'm not feeling particularly cheerful myself to-day."

"Monsieur l'Ambassadeur, I have been to the embassy to see you; and, learning where you had gone, I followed you."

"Well, that's very kind of you—very kind indeed. But what especial service can I render you?"

"It occurred to me that perhaps you might render me your assistance in finding Mrs. Asher."

Mr. Jackson looked at him keenly. "My dear young sir, if you will help me with your government to let in American wheat, I'll help you find Mrs. Asher. Everyone seems looking for her now, but I fear our task will be a difficult one."

The vicomte looked disappointed. "Your excellency does not know where she is?"

"I do not; and, to tell you the truth, my whole desire now is to forget Mrs. Asher," he added beneath his breath, as he thought of the letter he had read that morning.

"Then, your excellency, my mind is made up. I am going to sacrifice myself on the altar of duty."

"That is a very worthy intention. Might I inquire in which particular line the sacrifice is to be made?"

"Monsieur l'Ambassadeur, I am going to throw myself with fervor into a new movement. I am going to voice the discontent of the masses who are now dumb. In short, I am going to enter politics."

"Politics, my dear young sir, ought to be the ambition of every young man of talent and position. There would be much less cause for discontent in a country if the wishes of the masses could be voiced by people who really sympathize with them, instead of by professional demagogues and agitators."

"Your excellency has had wide experience of the representative system of government in America. Let me ask you frankly: Do you find France as truly representative as the country from which you come? Have no fear of offending me; I only ask for information, and would much appreciate your candid opinion."

"Since you put the question to me in that way, I must confess I have noticed certain differences between things here and at home."

"For instance?"

"Well, here the party that are in always seem to have far greater control of the electoral machinery than in America. Office at home is weakness, here it seems to be strength."

"Then there is less liberty here than in America?"

"In a sense, yes; and even when a change comes, it seems rather in name than fact. I am surprised to learn how little the machinery of government differs now from what it did under your former systems. The heads have changed, to be sure. There is, perhaps, less glitter; but, so far as the methods go, they are absolutely the same, and the prefect is armed with as much authority as ever before. Of course, I would not speak of my observations except you asked me; and I trust you will appreciate that I mention them in no offensive spirit."

"Monsieur l'Ambassadeur, I appreciate your frankness. We are both, I see, of the same way of thinking; and I trust that you will give me the privilege of coming to you and discussing these questions occasionally again."

"My dear sir, I shall always be happy to discuss any question with you. We dine at half-past seven o'clock, and we always have a place for our friends."

XXIII.

THE COMMUNIST, THE VICOMTE AND THE MAD MUSICIAN.

It is two evenings later. A thin, nervous-looking man is moving up and down the small apartment of a house in the environs of Paris. Every now and then he looks at the clock, and compares it with his watch. At the tinkling of the bell outside, he pauses. " Ah, there he is now," he exclaims. As he speaks, a slatternly servant woman ushers in the Vicomte de Dindon.

" When I wrote to crave this interview," began the visitor abruptly, "I explained my rank and position in the world. Here are letters which will confirm my statements."

" As head of the Socialistic party, I am scarcely one to whom these should appeal," replied the other, taking up the letters, however, and curiously glancing through them.

153

"Perhaps they will appeal to you when you learn in what connection they can be used; but I bring to you more than these. I bring to you an idea."

"Ah! that is better. Of what nature is your idea?"

"Listen. France, as you know, has been long engaged in changing the Sahara Desert into a sea by a canal. Again, as you know, the government has assisted the company with large subsidies. Perhaps you do not know that it has doctored up the report of the experts sent to investigate the slowness of the operations; and, to prevent the truth from coming out, has tried to buy the press of the entire country; further, there is scarcely a government official, inside or out of the Chambers, whose influence has not been engaged to support the scheme. It is merely a question of time when the facts will come out. You represent the masses —I, the aristocracy. My idea is that we unite our forces against the greatest scandal of modern times."

The socialist smiled ironically. "Supposing what you tell me be true, such a

combination would be the union of the dog
and the cat."

"Exactly. The dog and the cat that
unite to attack the rats."

"Ah! Monsieur le Vicomte is epigram-
matic."

"I am only practical."

"Prove it."

"By such a combination we win in the
coming elections."

"And after that?"

"We upset the government."

"And still again?"

"The country then can choose between
the ancient monarchy and the socialistic
republic."

"Has this idea been inspired by any
pretender—I should say, aspirant to the
throne?"

"It is all my own idea," replied the vicomte proudly. "It came to me suddenly.
All my best ideas are like that. Pouff! and it
was here," and the vicomte touched his brow.
"I will not deny," he continued, "that I
have been greatly encouraged in my plan
by my friend the American ambassador."

"By the American ambassador!" repeated the socialist in extreme surprise; and, for the first time, he seemed to give serious heed to his visitor.

"Yes; he assures me that this republic is nothing but a tyranny in disguise; that the fundamental principles of liberty are lacking; that men of my position and intelligence ought to come forward, and explain to the people their real needs. Of course, he only spoke in a general way, and without allusion to the Sahara Canal Company; but, naturally, that is what he meant."

"This is most remarkable. Are you quite sure it was the ambassador of the United States that told you this?"

"When I say the United States, I mean the United States," answered the young man curtly; "and my plan appealed to him."

"It does not appeal to me," said the other dryly. "I will admit the truth of much that you tell me about the rottenness of the present *régime;* but an attack upon it by allies so diametrically opposed is simply impossible."

"But you are irreconcilable—in fact, as well as in name," replied the vicomte. "As a party you are at one extreme; my party, let us admit, is at the other. I offer a suggestion that will bring the two extremes together. You spurn the assistance I offer, forgetting that all government is a compromise."

"Sir, the Socialistic party is the party of the future; your party is of the past. Old age can never assimilate with youth."

"I deny the analogy," said the vicomte; "measured by time, the monarchical principle is younger and fresher than that of socialism. You are absolutely the same as you were in Plato's time; and, while we can show ideal monarchies in actual existence, you can show only ideal republics in the brains of dreamers. Socialism is an island in the sea of ignorance that suffers no approach."

"Say rather socialism is a volcano that is destined to an early eruption, whose light will illumine the world."

"Say rather, socialism is a volcano whose last eruption illumined Paris with burning buildings, and landed many of its advocates in the ditch of Vincennes."

"Enough," cried the communist excitedly. "Do you mean to insult the dead?"

"On the contrary, I wish only to bring reason to the councils of the living."

"Then let me reply as of old—'*Timeo Danaos et dona ferentes.*'" The socialist bowed ironically. The vicomte bowed haughtily. "Very well," he said; "if that is your view, I will draw my visit to a close. One of these days you may regret not having listened to the Vicomte de Dindon." Thereupon the vicomte took his hat and withdrew.

As he drove homeward the moon was shining brightly. It was a hot, stuffy night, with clouds of dust extending the length of the long straight road. Innumerable carts laden with provisions were traveling the same course. Their drivers were either asleep within, or astride one of the great gray docile horses that in single file trod the well-worn path leading to that immense mouth—Paris. Food of every description that the imagination of man could conjure up appeared in those carts—cheeses and poultry, meats and vegetables, all heaped in an abundance that oppressed the beholder.

"Of what use is this continual round of repletion?" thought the vicomte. "Do men eat only that they may live to eat again?" The reflection sickened him. He felt irritable and forlorn, recognizing that he had hardly shown much tact in his interview, and yet not willing to admit the fact even to himself. He found excuse for his irritability in everything on and along the road—in the dust, in the poplar trees on each side, in the very houses whose fronts shone whitely behind infrequent lanterns; and never having felt the pangs of hunger, he was especially aggrieved at the long line of innocent carts that, like wheeled cornucopias, were rolling plenty to the great city.

It was with a sense of relief that he saw the lights ahead becoming brighter, and that peculiar luminousness of the sky that, like an aureole, surrounds Paris at night. Not till arriving at the Arc de Triomphe could the contrast between the gloomy outskirts and the city be fully appreciated; then Paris burst upon him in all its grandeur. Owing to the heat everyone seemed to be abroad; and down the broad avenue the lamps of oncoming vehicles made, as far as the eye could reach, a river of fire. On passing the Rond Point the sound of music reached his ear. It was scarcely yet his hour for retiring, so he bade the cabman await his return; and, descending among the crowds of idlers, he crossed the gardens of the Champs Élysées, finally entering one of those little open-air concert halls known as *café chantants.*

A small man, with a comical red face and a high hat, was singing a song which the vicomte had already heard a couple of hundred times at least. The little man was succeeded in due course by a stout lady, whose smile would have been more seductive but for a couple of little black patches on each side of a wide mouth. It was all very wearisome; and, having consumed his ice, the vicomte sank his head into his hand, and lapsed into reverie.

How it was I cannot explain, save it be that
his drive had wearied him; but the faces
about him gradually became indistinct, the
lights faded, and his reverie merged into a
fitful slumber, with the eh-la-la, tra-la-la of
the fair performer, and the jingle-jangle of
the accompanying piano making an odd
medley in his ear.

As he slept, the music must have given
direction to the action of his mind. He
dreamed a curious dream of two angels—a
good angel and a bad—struggling for the
mastery of a soul; the angels being different and distinct strains of music. At last
a torrent of sound seemed to blot out the
good angel. He awoke with a start. The
place was in confusion—men were gesticulating about him, while on the stage a
couple of gendarmes were forcibly remov-
ing a struggling form. Then, as he stu-
pidly gazed about him, the smiling lady,
who, it would seem, had retreated during
the trouble, reappeared and apologized for
the break in the performance. Turning to
the occupant of the next seat for an
explanation, the vicomte learned that the

pianist who had been accompanying the singer must have gone mad, as his conduct and his music had, without any warning, become very peculiar. "It was as if some horrible thought carried him away, till, losing all control of himself, he gave expression to the tumult raging in his breast. Poor devil! that is what absinthe brings these musicians to—otherwise he never would be in a *café chantant.*"

The vicomte rose and paid his score. Strange as it may seem, the incident made a deep impression on him. All night long, aye, and for days after, his dream kept recurring to him with the contradictory strains that he then seemed to have heard; the one grand, solemn, and impressive, the other weirdly sparkling and vivacious, yet combined with a fantastic sensuality that would have turned a hermit mad. Do what he would, he could not shake off the idea that they had some particular pertinency to himself. In some ways he might seem the soul that was being contended for: the angel of good personifying the craving for an active, honorable career;

the angel of evil, the circumstances that dragged him under. For the vicomte was one of those men who earnestly desire occupation for its own sake—who feel the need of a career as a sustaining prop in life. The trouble was he desired, like so many others, to begin at the big end; while his training and experience completely unfitted him for either end.

His desires for a career were intensified by Mrs. Asher's absence; and, realizing that he had cut himself off from any prospects of a political nature, he became a prey to an extreme misanthropy, through which that mad musician's discords vibrated with strange meanings.

XXIV.

WITH the close of the London season,
Mrs. de Trow hied her to Homburg.
Here she now was, fluttering about as
usual, organizing picnics, and getting up all
species of entertainments, the head and
front of a *coterie* of which Lady Summerset de Vere and the Princess de Xamarinda
were shining lights. Indeed, Mrs. de Trow
had but one cause of regret; namely, the
extreme wariness of a certain great personage usually in much demand in Homburg.
But for this she consoled herself with an
aged grand duke, whose waning eyesight
and scarcity of molars made him a safe
recipient of her confidences touching the
tender passion.

Mr. de Trow, however, found Homburg
less to his tastes. In the first place, there
was no Palais Royal with its shop windows to relieve his tedium; then the
waters which his wife insisted on his imbib-

ing (because, being at Homburg, he must do as others did), disagreed with his digestion; and lastly, the surveillance over the grand duke increased in irksomeness each day, by reason of the growing audacity of other fair countrywomen of his who were ever on the alert to entice the aged lion from Mrs. de Trow's picnics and confidences to their own. The crowning feature of Mr. de Trow's discomfort, however, was that his wife, when in London, had been presented with a small Dandy Dinmont terrier, upon which it became the province of de Trow to attend. And yet, to such a degree do the noblest of us succumb to routine, that the poor man was more ready to repine than to rejoice when the little spoiled darling, breaking through the fond restraints that hedged him in, strayed away one night, and, indulging in some unspeakable orgies of a gluttonous nature with other canines of his acquaintance, came home on the morrow to expire in the arms of his friends. This sad event was duly recorded in Mr. de Trow's diary under the date of August 19th. A gallop through the pages of this diary will not only give an insight into the routine of life of our exiles generally in Homburg, but we shall also find entries big with import to those with whom we are more immediately concerned.

"August 31.   Maneuvers of the German Army began to-day. Drove to review with Mrs. O'Hagan, as Dora insisted on going with Xamarindas. Awful woman; squeezed me up in the corner of the carriage till I could scarcely breathe, and talked in the highest key of her grievances, which are too numerous to repeat. Poor Summerset wasn't as lucky with his *belle mere* as Xam. She enters all his unfortunate adventures on the turf in her diary and to-day in the carriage he was compelled to listen to quotations. Could anything be more dreary for a holiday! Reflections on German army. They have a peculiar way of stepping; wear smart uniforms; and, when they charge, shout 'hoch.'

"September 3. Awful row between Mrs. O'Hagan and her daughter, because the latter did not invite her to a dinner for *the* Prince. The fact is the Prince positively forbade her being included, on the score of her effect on his nerves. Mrs. O'Hagan got into a fearful rage when she was told this, reproached her daughter for her lack of filial consideration in not insisting on her presence, tearfully recited the number of times she had paid her 'wretched, knock-kneed, and degenerate son-in-law's gambling debts' (as if poor Xam had anything to do with her exclusion), and tragically wound up with the reminder that, to allow her daughter the income she enjoyed, she, Mrs. O'Hagan, had scrimped herself to a degree that involved the sacrifice of her *brusse-à-dent*. Her daughter delicately hinted the deprivation was scarcely a hardship, as her dental machinery was removable and usually polished with a towel; whereupon the fond parent collapsed in hysterics on the carpet.

"September 5. Invitation from grand duke to castle in Bohemia, from October 1st to 15th. Boar hunting. Of course it's in the nature of a command; but how I do wish it had been to shoot rooks with a pea rifle! Far preferable as a sport—no danger, and your gun never kicks.

"September 8. Invitations by floods to other châteaus for autumn. It's got wind, I fancy, we're going to stay with grand duke. *Le succès rapporte le succès.* We'll have only to pick this season.

"September 10. Dinner at the Kursaal. Conversation turned on Mrs. Asher. General wonder expressed as to her whereabouts. Later in evening a man mysteriously drew me to one side; and, under promise of secrecy, inquired whether I had ever heard the report that she was the subject of a frenzied pursuit by a discarded lover who had avowed the amiable intention of taking her life. There's something mysterious about that woman. She's just the kind to be connected with some awful tragedy. I feel it in my bones.

"September 18. Talking about stories; heard good one about Princess de Xamarinda's stately repose of manner. First thing her husband is said to have observed to her after marriage was: 'My dear, as

Miss O'Hagan of Hoshkosh, it was quite natural that your voice should be pitched in a high key, and that your tongue should wag as loud and as continuously as that of the bell in one of your Western locomotives; but let me remind you, now you're my wife, it's different, and a Princess of Xamarinda is supposed to maintain a stately reserve.' Before every sentence now she inwardly counts three, but sometimes the restraint becomes intolerable, and in these cases she closets herself with her friend Lady Summerset de Vere who has been repressing her own voice in some similar manner, and they secretly indulge together in a good old-fashioned American yell. I wish I could induce Dora to count three before every sentence—but when she reacted—O Lord!

"September 20. *The* Prince left to-day. Must confess, my appreciation of his ability has reached its acme. For a man to dodge Dora for five whole weeks when she has set her mind upon him, and then to get away scot free, proves him to be gifted beyond the ordinary run of men.

"September 21. Maracovini and English secretary turned up, swearing at their respective ambassadors for keeping them all summer at their posts, and making them return in ten days. Report something strange likely soon to come out about Mr. Jackson; also report unusual activity among the socialists, and possible risings of the populace over these Sahara Canal disclosures. These French people are never satisfied. They set up a republic one day, and then set to work to pull it down the next.

"September 22. Unexpected scene to-day between Dora and Xam's mother-in-law, the O'Hagan. It seems that the latter got it into her head that the reason the Prince had forbidden her presence at her daughter's table was because he confounded her in some way with Dora. Dora naturally resented this version as unflattering, and retorted that Mrs. O'Hagan was actually responsible for the Prince's departure from Homburg. Thereupon the O'Hagan flung in her face a reported observation of the Prince—that having dodged

Dora during the latter part of the London season, it was rather hard to have to begin all over again here. You should have seen Dora rear up. I never had any idea of the reserve power of that woman. She reared up, and then she fell on the unhappy O'Hagan like a carload of brick—described her face as being more highly colored than her stories, and added that if the Prince had recently desisted in his attentions to any of our countrywomen, it was because of such representatives of the nation as Mrs. O'H.—who disgraced her sex by her conduct, robbed gray hair of its dignity by a wig, and introduced into polite society the manners of a charwoman. There's nothing like standing right up to these people. The O'Hagan actually wilted into tears, and begged for curaçoa to restore her shattered nerves. She's a terror, that woman. Just to think of her being at large! At home, no one ever heard of her till her daughter's marriage. Yet, here she forces herself everywhere. Indeed, the more I see of European society, the higher opinion I begin to entertain of our own. With us a certain degree of refinement is essential; in Europe, it seems to count for nothing; and, so long as people have money and plenty of assurance, every barrier eventually falls."

One more entry and then we have done. It is under the head of September 30, and many important events are to hang upon it. "Grand visit of reconciliation from Mrs. O'Hagan. Dora and she as thick as thieves again. For some reason best known to herself charged all the trouble to Summerset de Vere; went on to observe that with that young man before her eyes, she has grown to have an unutterable contempt for Englishmen, who have no respect for woman's feelings, contrasting them most unfavorably in this respect with the men of Rome—where she had spent the preceding winter—to whom she went on to attribute all the manly virtues and sentiments.

"The effect on Dora was noticeable. I read in her eyes that she suddenly remembered there was one last remaining field of conquest."

That this prognostication of Mr. de

Trow's was not unwarranted was soon proved. "Percival, dear," lisped the lady next morning, "I've noticed that you have not been looking well lately. It sometimes occurs to me that the life we have been leading is not the best for either of us. I have therefore decided that, after we leave the grand duke's, we will pass the rest of the autumn visiting about in the country, and afterward——"

"And afterward that we go to Rome?" hazarded her husband.

"Why, yes, but how did you guess it?"

"Oh, never mind," replied her spouse grimly.

"I am so anxious to behold the Colosseum, and the Vatican, and all the other emblems of a glorious past," continued the lady. "You know the adage, 'See Rome, and then die.'"

"I thought the adage referred to Naples," said Mr. de Trow ironically.

"Now, Percival, I know you're angry and wish to quarrel, but I shall not give you the chance; you have no appreciation for anything outside of the Palais Royal.

As for me, I have a strange curiosity about the works of these ancient Romans; you must admit we ought to see these before we die."

"And at the same time work the grand passion racket, and the sweet communion of souls, for the benefit of the modern Romans."

"Percival, I really believe you're jealous of poor little me," lisped the lady, as she put her pink finger nail between her lips and pensively regarded her husband.

"No, I'm not a bit jealous—quite the contrary, in fact," retorted the gentleman; and he spoke with a decisiveness that showed he meant what he said. Thus passed the summer of his discontent.

XXV.

A STARTLING ENCOUNTER WITH THE POLICE
AND AN UNEXPECTED ARRIVAL FROM
DIANAPOLIS, THE HEAD CENTER OF
DIVORCE.

BACK in August some time Mr. Jackson had offered the second secretaryship to the son of a life-long friend. The position had been gladly accepted by the young man; but illness was offered as an excuse for his failure to present himself at his post. The month of October was now well advanced, and he still delayed his coming. Had Mr. Jackson desired to take the vacation to which he was entitled, the absence of the second secretary might have caused inconvenience; for, by his own departure, an unfair proportion of work would have been imposed on Mr. Pettigrew.

Mr. Jackson, however, had no desire to absent himself. The political sky, erewhile so clear, was overclouded, and an interpellation of the government on the subject of the Sahara Canal scheme was threatened. Besides, he had taken a small but attractive hotel, whose bit of garden, with

its trees and statues, offered many of the
charms of a country abode, and where he
was far more comfortable than he would
likely have been in any summer caravansary.
There are beautiful walks and drives in
the environs of Paris, delightful little cafés
along the Seine, nooks of unexpected sylvan
beauty in the Bois de Boulogne, and charming islets in its lakes. Men, in blue jean
sailor suits of a theatrical cut, row you
about the lake in boats that strangely recall
a ship of Christopher Columbus' time without the masts; and, as you float along, you
get irretrievably mixed up with swans, and
geese, and bourgeois wedding parties in
black dress coats and tulle. All these
sights Mr. and Mrs. Jackson exploited, nor
were they lonely because the great world
of fashion had deserted Paris. Indeed,
the cessation of their social duties enabled
them to indulge in the quiet home life
which was so dear to both, and to make
acquaintance with a class of people whom,
in the rush of the season, it would have
been difficult to know. Thus young men
and women in the schools of art and medi-

cine found a hearty welcome at their embassy.

Occasionally of an evening, too, the dentist and his wife would drop in after dinner; when, if the weather permitted, there were placed on the balcony four large rocking chairs especially brought from America. Thereupon all would indulge in what they playfully distinguished as a good, old-fashioned American rock; Mrs. Jackson and Mrs. Lovejoy perhaps talking baby on one side (for Mrs. Lovejoy presented a grateful world with at least one proof per year that *her* marriage was no failure), while Mr. Jackson and Mr. Lovejoy discussed the development of dentistry in Latin countries. Thus engaged, they would watch the domed and spired city at their feet, darkling in the twilight. Or sometimes of an evening, Mr. Lovejoy would call for Mr. Jackson to join him in a walk on the boulevards; when, if frivolously inclined, they would stop at a café for an ice. This habit was regarded rather askance by their wives; and, as we shall see, not always without reason. The anniversary of the decease of a well-known agitator oc-curring about this time, it had been chosen by his sympathizers for a demonstration against the government. Though this intention had aroused considerable uneasiness in official circles, the day passed off quietly. After dinner Mr. Lovejoy happened to call on the ambassador, and proposed a stroll. Mr. Jackson assented; so they sauntered down the boulevards, and subsequently took seats before a café, in the neighborhood of the Porte St. Martin. Here they found the excitement at fever heat. Everyone inside and outside the café appeared to be engaged in a linguistic duel with his neighbor, and all were gesticulating at the fiercest rate.

Mr. Jackson surveyed them with a smile of quiet amusement. "To judge from the way these people go on," he exclaimed, "they ought to have a cord around their waists, with an organ-grinder at the other end. That's the only thing they require to make the resemblance complete."

"They have certainly made but little advance over here in dental surgery," said

Mr. Lovejoy, whose thoughts continually reverted to his profession. "The most painfully amusing sight I ever beheld was an elderly French gentleman who wore an antiquated set of Evans' sixes instead of Smith's imperial self-adjusting fives."

"I don't understand," replied the envoy.

"Excuse me, sir; I allude to what a layman would call his artificial teeth. You see, they were a size too large for him, and, being moreover, of a primitive make, they kept his lips extended in a manner that your reference to the simian family and their grimaces vaguely recalled."

"Oh, I didn't see the point," said our representative, laughing; "but, dear me, what is the meaning of all this?"

Distant shouts and yells were suddenly heard down the boulevard. Rising to their feet, as all the rest about them did, our two friends paid their score (as all the rest did not). I am sorry to say their honesty was not rewarded as it should have been; for, while they were waiting for their change, the waiters suddenly emerged in a body; and, sweeping chairs, bottles, and tables in one indiscriminate mass to the interior, pulled down the shutters and put out the lights.

" Well, upon my word," said Mr. Jackson, " if that isn't the most contemptible expedient I ever saw to rob one of twenty-five cents change."

" It reminds me of an experience I once had in Arkansas," said Mr. Lovejoy. "I was just presenting my bill for an operation on an upper bi-cuspid——"

The reminiscence was destined to remain unrelated. A confused rabble, whose approach had been unnoticed by our two friends in their surprise at the closing of the café, was swarming around them on every side. They were crying, "Down with the Jews!" (the Jews were held to be largely responsible for the Sahara Canal scheme), and after them, sweeping them along as chaff, came a line of *sergents de ville*, extending across the entire roadway of the street with swords drawn. Never did our envoy forget the sight of those police, as they advanced in their long hooded coats, the light flashing on their naked blades and their dark saturnine faces, each with its fiercely twisted mustache. There was something of the hired bravo in their appearance— something so much more sinister than in that of an ordinary platoon of honest locust-swinging bobbies, that our envoy stood rooted to the ground. Before he was aware of it, a point was at his breast, and a rough hand on his throat. The fact disagreeably recalled him to his senses. "What do you mean, sir?" he exclaimed, as he shook himself free. "I think you will find that you have made an egregious mistake."

"*Sacré Anglais,*" cried the *sergent* fiercely.

"*Pas Anglais,*" replied Mr. Jackson, more soothingly. "*Américain ambassadeur.*"

"*Américain ambassadeur?*" mimicked the hireling; "*mais que faites-vous donç dans cette galère-ci?*"

"How?" ejaculated our envoy interrogatively; for, while in the repose of his study he could read French fairly well, his acquaintance with the language was not

equal to the comprehension of sudden linguistic bursts; but, at that moment, the
officer spied the dentist struggling to his
feet, for he had been knocked down in the
rush, and, turning away from Mr. Jackson,
seized him with both hands by the hair.

"And this man, is he also an American
ambassador?" inquired the gendarme ironically.

"Non, ça c'est ung de mes amis, dentist,
bung garçon;" and Mr. Jackson, to demon-
strate the pacific profession of his comrade,
so far yielded to the situation as to make a
pantomimic display suggestive of drawing
the cork from a bottle, though it was intended to apply more strictly to the extrac-
tion of teeth.

In the meantime, the crowd and their
pursuers had swept on, leaving the *gendarme* with his distinguished captives on
the sidewalk. The incident had taken Mr.
Jackson so much by surprise that it had
not, as yet, occurred to him to show his
card. This he now did. The *sergent*
took it suspiciously, read it in the light of
a lamp-post attentively; and, though retain-

ing it, expressed his abject apologies for the mistake, further offering to conduct the gentlemen to a cab stand—a suggestion which the judge finally accepted.

The incident would probably have made more impression on Mr. Jackson's mind but for a very unexpected event which had happened during his absence from home that same evening, and connected with which was a circumstance that so engrossed Mr. Pettigrew's mind as to leave him with little interest in his superior's misadventure. This event was the unannounced arrival of the young gentleman who had been appointed several months before to the post of second secretary. Of all things, Mr. Pettigrew most disliked surprises; and this young man gave Mr. Pettigrew a surprise by hunting him up when he could not find the ambassador at his home. Mr. Pettigrew disliked also being disturbed after a quiet dinner, particularly in the interior of his own abode, which was of a less luxurious character than he wished it to be imagined. But what Mr. Pettigrew disliked the most was a young man of the free-and-easy,

breezy manner which this young man possessed.   Nevertheless, Mr. Pettigrew being
surprised into opening his door, was compelled to admit his visitor after hearing
who he was, and to offer him, as a substitute for a more lavish hospitality, a chair.
This the young man took, and proceeded to
give Mr. Pettigrew a description of his
voyage over and his opinion of Paris after
three hours' acquaintance; to draw a com-
parison between the policies of Europe and
America; and to pass a hurried commentary
on French architecture, which built houses
five stories high without lifts.   His visitor
pausing for a moment to catch his breath,
Mr. Pettigrew availed himself of the
opportunity to inqure into his long delay
in reaching his post, whereupon the young
man adopted an extremely sentimental air.

"Thereby, O Pettigrew, hangs a tale.
A few days after I was offered this post,
when, in fact, I was making my prepara-
tions for departure, I fell ill—really ill—
and was laid up for some three weeks.
On my recovery from my physical ailment,
I succumbed to one of a different kind.

O Pettigrew, did you ever fall in love? in love to a degree that, for a smile from your charmer, you'd be willing to walk out of a third-story window backward, cross Niagara on a cobweb, or hang by your eyelashes to Not-a-dam spire?"

"I must confess," returned Mr. Pettigrew, in his stateliest accents, and with a growing dislike for his forward young visitor, "I can hardly imagine myself allowing my feelings to carry me away to such an extent."

"Then, my friend, you have never known what it is to love. How doth the poet say? —'Better to have loved and lost, than never to have loved at all.' Pettigrew, I lost my rest, my peace of mind, and what the philosopher calls happiness. It came about in this wise. The day before I was finally to leave for Paris, I stopped at a hotel to learn the times of starting of the east bound trains. Now, Dianapolis, as perhaps you are aware, is the banner city for divorces; and the hotels are usually full of those that seek relief from matrimony's yoke. Having obtained a time-table, I was departing,

when, passing through the halls, I saw a
face that bewitched me. On inquiry, all I
could learn about the owner was her name,
and that she was there for a divorce. From
the moment I saw her I forgot all else;
for, Pettigrew, there is a chord in my
nature strangely sensitive to romance and
that is always touched by a woman's seeking a divorce. Like Ulysses, I gave up my
sailing and haunted the corridors of the
hotel day after day. Every expedient,
however, to make an impression failed. I
sent her cards and letters, concealed in
roses, craving an interview and describing
the honorable nature of my intentions.
The flowers were kept, the letters returned.
Finally I explained the glorious career
diplomacy extended to me; insinuating
that while only second secretary now, I
would soon supersede the first secretary,
that's you, and perhaps eventually take
Mr. Jackson's place. The extraordinary
part is that the more I dwelt on these particulars, the more she seemed to avoid me.
In fact, after this I only beheld her thrice
again, and she never vouchsafed me a

glance. At last one day I learned that she had left for parts unknown with her decree in her pocket, having rushed things through I suppose by some pull on the judge and by squaring the counsel on the opposing side. Then of Pettigrew I was left with nothing but regret and a fleeting impression I had secured of her with my kodak. Only a photo—Pettigrew—only a photo—but I had it developed, colored and enlarged and wear it over my heart as a talisman and a charm against dyspepsia. What would you give for a glance at her countenance?"

Mr. Pettigrew did not make a high bid for the privilege, but he expressed sufficient interest to cause the other to draw a photograph from his pocket. Mr. Pettigrew took it, started violently, and turned pale. It bore an unmistakable resemblance to Mrs. Asher. Fortunately the young man noticed nothing, having turned away to conceal a sigh.

"Her departure recalled me to my duties," the visitor continued; "and having no further cause for delay, I came, and here I am. By the way, as I see we're to be

intimate, suppose I inaugurate the friendship by ringing for a bottle of champagne,
after which, I'll give you just ten minutes
to put me up to my new work, fully
describe the life, tell me who your friends
are, and what are the latest quotations on
the Paris Bourse."

The effect on Mr. Pettigrew's nerves of
these various disclosures, professions, and
proposals, was not dissimilar to that from
a series of sharp electric shocks. Before
he could fairly recover himself, Mr. Jackson was announced. It happened that his
course home from the Boulevards lay in
Mr. Pettigrew's direction; and, when he
arrived near the latter's house, it occurred
to him he might as well stop and explain
his adventure. Between our representative's surprise at finding his second secretary, and the first secretary's surprise at the
confidence just elicited, the adventure with
the police shrank into insignificance.

XXVI.

Possibly Mr. Breeze gave a different version of his delay to his chief; but what this was need not be recorded, as Mr. Breeze is not destined to remain long with us.

The chief characteristic of Mr. Breeze was his changeableness. Having swept into Paris, he soon swept out. Indeed, the duration of his diplomatic experience was limited to just four days. Learning that he would be expected to copy state documents in a careful hand, and that the opportunities of speculating in corner lots in Paris were limited, he suddenly announced a preference for a scamper through the Holy Land, which had for its somewhat contradictory objects the locating of Solomon's Temple and the search for natural gas. Thus he departed as he came, but not before Mr. Pettigrew had learned all he knew about the original of the photograph, which was extremely little. Mr. Pettigrew felt convinced the picture he had been shown was that of Mrs. Asher, although the name of Mrs. Ferdinand Schultze was that given by Mr. Breeze. This difference of designation, however, might be accounted for by some previous marriage; and he finally decided to write to a lawyer of his acquaintance, who had lately moved to a town in the neighborhood of Dianapolis, and who was further under some trifling obligations to him. Mr. Pettigrew begged this gentleman to put himself into communication with Mrs. Schultze's lawyer in Dianapolis, and to learn from him, or from any other source, all the particulars ascertainable about her. To show the degree to which Mr. Pettigrew's interest was aroused, Mr. Pettigrew begged his friend to spare no expense in his search.

The conduct of his second secretary pained and chagrined Mr. Jackson excessively. While he had enjoyed too brief an acquaintance with him to admit of his detecting any faults in the young man's moral character, yet, for the father's sake, he regretted the son's vacillation, and was ready to make excuses for it.

"I sometimes imagine that I have found a logical explanation of young Breeze's departure," he observed one day to his wife.

"You see he was reared in the hard-ware business and he found the require-ments too dissimilar. I suppose the smartest of your diplomats here couldn't run a hardware store if dropped into it suddenly and I begin to wonder whether the reverse is not true. Small things, too, get to have such a meaning; why, here I have been worrying all day over a mere change of manner on the part of the minister of foreign affairs. I am not sure, too, whether it may not have existed only in my imagination, but this morning it struck me that he was less cordial than usual. How would you like me to throw up my position here and try for the nom-ination for the governorship? I think I could get it for the asking."

The eyes of the lady brightened. "I will not influence you, Samuel; but, when you are prepared to go, I am ready."

Mr. Jackson was by no means a man of suspicious nature, but that his instincts were keen is proved by his receiving less than a month later a semi-official document from the State Department in Washington. This hinted as delicately as possible that the French government had expressed itself as dissatisfied with certain remarks attributed to our representative—remarks to the effect that the present order in France, viewed from an American standpoint, but inadequately filled the conceptions of a popular government; and, further, that an improvement could only be effected by a combination of the various elements of discontent in the country against it.

These observations had been largely quoted by the opposing parties, who were thus furnished with a fresh weapon of attack: namely, the unfavorable criticism upon the newest democracy by the official representative of the oldest. The government had refused at first to take any notice of the noise these reports occasioned, believing Mr. Jackson to have been simply misquoted. But however natural such an inference might seem, it had been lately rebutted by the discovery of his frequenting cafés well known as the rendez-vous of socialists. The secretary of state, after reciting these complaints, ridiculed the idea of their resting on any substantial basis; still he closed his letter with the suggestion that Mr. Jackson should remember the sensitiveness of the people to whom he was accredited, and endeavor, as far as possible, to avoid political subjects in the present critical condition of affairs.

Mr. Jackson read the communication with astonishment.

"But, I haven't spoken a word on politics since I have been here," he muttered to himself. "No, not a word, except—oh, yes! except to that young vicomte. Yes, I remember now," he continued, as his conversation at the Quai d'Orsay recurred to his memory. "He must have misconstrued what I said to him and have repeated it. Then it is enlarged on till it reaches the government through its spies. Finally, to cap the climax, the café, where they forgot to give me my change that night, turns out to be a center of · agitation. I see it all. But it's an outrage that a government that pretends to be a sensible one should give ear to such reports."

Mr. Jackson was inordinately moved. Admitting that he had been indiscreet, he felt that his conduct had been spied upon and misrepresented. The pettiness of the whole affair was to a man of his nature especially galling. Make any explanation? Certainly not. It would be beneath him. There was but one course.

"Mr. Pettigrew," he said, when that gentleman answered his summons, a few minutes later, "I am going to send in my resignation;" and he proceeded to relate his grievance.

As Mr. Pettigrew listened he was dazed by the prospect before him. If his chief carried out his intention, he, the secretary, would be left as *chargé* at an increased salary and probably for an indefinite period. Yet Mr. Pettigrew was proof against these temptations, and be it said to his credit, he loyally endeavored to dissuade his chief from hasty action. Mr. Jackson had a certain stubbornness of disposition that argument sometimes rather intensified than abated, and he forthwith cabled to his government to learn when it would suit their convenience to accept his resignation.

This communication proved as surprising as it was annoying to the State Department. It proved surprising because, in repeating the complaints of the French government, the department had put the matter with great delicacy, and merely in a suggestive manner with regard to the future course of our representative.

The reason why his dispatch proved irritating to the department can be inferred. One of its diplomatic appointees in South America, by endeavoring to carry out the pacific scheme of reciprocity, had brought us to the verge of war with the country to which he was accredited. Another representative, through too pronounced a tendency to primitive methods of settling international disputes, had seriously strained our relations with a second South American government. The ambassador to England had erred on the other hand in making himself popular in the only country where one of our representatives should not be popular : while Sicily had insisted upon the recall of another, when she discovered that in a speech in Congress he had alluded to her sovereign as a brigand. Thereupon he was withdrawn and offered to Russia, which in turn had showed him the cold shoulder for no better reason, poor man, than that he had been rejected by a nation inferior in diplomatic status. His case was a cruel one. He had sold his house and household effects in America and was now a wanderer over Europe, for whom the administration were at their wit's end to find a place.

To have Mr. Jackson throw up his post, on top of all these perplexities, was to give color to charges of the opposition that the foreign policy of the government had not been administered with the glitter-ing success its exponents claimed for it. There was yet one far graver objection to

Mr. Jackson's resignation. If he resigned, he would very likely return to his own country and to his native State. Here the nomination to the governorship was soon due, and would probably gravitate toward him. The duration of the gubernatorial term was three years, the end of which would leave him, if elected (and of this there would be little doubt, if he ran), a dangerous luminary at a period disagreeably close to the next presidential nomination. For Mr. Jackson, while naturally being of the party in power, yet belonged to the opposite wing, and was therefore more feared by the administration than had he belonged to the other side.

Mr. Jackson, too, had been steadily growing in popularity during his absence; and, following our custom of starting the search for the next President as soon as one has been seated, talk was springing up about Mr. Jackson's fitness for the chair, while such flattering terms as "The Grand Old American," and the "Gladstone of the West" were being applied to him with greater frequency. The judge at home would be a white elephant on the hands of the administration. How should the white elephant be kept away, if only till after the nomination for the governorship could be given to someone else? The most natural course was to withdraw the too popular English ambassador and offer his post to Mr. Jackson; but the administration was not yet ready to face the confession of failure which this would imply, and reserved it as a last resort.

After long deliberation and several cabinet meetings, it was resolved to appeal to Mr. Jackson's patriotism (always a wise course when you desire to use a man to your own advantage); and, explaining the ill-effects on the administration of his resignation, to beg him to withhold it: if he insisted on leaving his post, however, to urge him to do so under pretext of taking a vacation for three months, which would throw him just outside of gubernatorial possibilities. Mr. Jackson, in the meanwhile, had had time to reconsider his action. He was one of those rare men who can as readily see an error in themselves as in others, and was, moreover, always willing to acknowledge a fault. Nevertheless, he read between the lines of the dispatch the desire to keep him in Europe, and appreciated the motive.

"I am quite ready to admit," he wrote back, "that I was a trifle hasty ; and, since you appeal to my patriotism, I will withhold my resignation for the present, and take a brief vacation, which I will spend in Italy. There I will decide whether I can do my country more good by retaining the French mission or by going home and devoting myself to local politics."

Some five days later, Mr. and Mrs. Jackson started for Rome with the Lovejoys, who begged to accompany them on a sort of reconnoitering tour, since business had not proved as brisk in Paris as they had anticipated.

Mr. and Mrs. de Trow, after their round of visits in the country, also started for Rome. They stopped in Paris long enough to allow madame to arrange for leave of absence in behalf of Signor de Maracovini and the English attaché, who, she insisted, should accompany her. Thus the clans were concentrating at the Eternal City, leaving Mr. Pettigrew in charge of the embassy, as a reward for the true magnanimity of his conduct.

A couple of days after the judge's departure, Mr. Pettigrew received a reply from his friend in Dianapolis. While this left little doubt that Mrs. Schultze and Mrs. Asher were one, the matter of that lady's antecedents was not explained with the fullness he had hoped. So he wrote back to secure, if possible, further particulars. Having done this, it occurred to him to put himself in correspondence with the American consul at Cairo, in the hope that that official might be possessed of any information touching her sojourn in Egypt. Then, having set in operation all this machinery, he learned a few days later that Mrs. Asher had again turned up in Europe; and, of all places in the world, at Rome.

XXVII.

YES, Mrs. Asher the divine, Mrs. Asher the mysterious, again burst upon an admiring world without so much as a hint of her coming. And what more appropriate stage could the fair young widow have selected for her reappearance? Life consists in agreeable contrasts, she often observed; and she was one of the few who acted up to her principles. There was much, too, in Rome that, apart from religious sentiment, fascinated her: its glorious history, its wealth of art, its flavor of asceticism, and its antiquity. Consequently, no one resented more than she the efforts Rome was making to modernize herself; and in this regard, I think, Mrs. Asher showed her sense of fitness.

What right has Rome to wake up and cut new streets? What right has she to tear down her historic buildings, to break up her ancient gardens, and to lay bare her classic shrines? There is an absolute immodesty about unbaring what time has clothed. These belong to history, and not alone to Rome herself. But alas! she is giving up her supremacy as queen of the past to become a fifth-rate modern city, bankrupting herself in the foolish effort. Over her cheap improvements in brick and mortar the noble dome of St. Peter's towers, a relic of more glorious days; priests and monks flit like shadows among swagger officers; while the *table d'hôte* gongs at the different hotels drown the bells for vespers, and the sweet strains of music from the Pincian hill.

There ought surely to be left some quiet nook, where the troubled soul may find repose. Possibly the most anachronistic development of the day was the performance actually going on here within the sacred precincts of the Colosseum, namely, the American Wild West Show. It is an odd coincidence that, not very long ago, when the same show on its first visit to the Eternal City was astonishing the inhabitants, the " Fall of Rome," was the most attractive feature of a performance in New York, under the auspices of the renowned and late Mr. Barnum.

Yet, in spite of the sensation Mrs. Asher's arrival created, it was not altogether flattering to that lady. Her abrupt departure from Paris was recalled; and, in this connection, the gossip of her having paid the Vicomte de Dindon's debts was revived. Roman society held a little aloof; and, worse than this, it was said that the master of ceremonies was half inclined to drop her name from the list of applicants for presentation at the first court ball. Her surprise at finding the Jacksons in the city was probably less genuine than her annoyance at discovering that the Lovejoys were attached to their suite. Nevertheless, Mrs. Asher immediately secured the best rooms in the hotel where the ambassador and his wife were domiciled, and had her luggage transferred thither.

"To think we should all meet again here," she exclaimed to Mrs. Jackson. "There is something providential about it."

Mrs. Jackson looked at the lady askance.

She resented being taken possession of, as it were, in such a way.

"I hope you are quite cured of your indisposition," she said. "It was in the nature of dyspepsia, was it not?"

"Oh, no; my heart, you know, has an unnatural action; but the simple life in my quiet retreat, the bracing air and the strict regimen I subjected myself to, have completely rebuilt me. By the way, are you also going to be presented next Wednesday evening? It is the first ball of the season. I do hope you are. It is as well, you know, to see as many agreeable phases of life as possible when one is traveling."

"Though Mr. Jackson is to have a private interview with the king, he thought it becoming to send in our names," replied Mrs. Jackson. "He has a great regard for Italy, and considers that its form of government approaches nearer to a republic than that of any other kingdom in Europe."

"Ah, poor Italy! But it is not what it was. With the Pope a prisoner, and the great ceremonies of the Church abolished, its glory has sadly departed. You know, I look at things from a Roman Catholic standpoint."

"And I look at them from the standpoint of a Methodist," said Mrs. Jackson stoutly.

"I have often thought," was Mrs. Asher's diplomatic reply, "that the real Church should embrace all forms of Christianity; so that Methodists and Roman Catholics should feel that they belong to one fold."

"When that day comes, I shall cease to be a Christian," Mrs. Jackson was about to observe, but she controlled her tongue, reproaching herself for her lack of warmth in meeting the advances of the wife of her husband's old friend.

Mrs. Asher was also quick to resume her acquaintance with Mrs. de Trow. "Oh, how happy, happy I am to fall again among you all!" she exclaimed impulsively to that lady. "The more I live, the more I appreciate that it is our friendships alone that make life tolerable."

"True," said Mrs. de Trow, "but why did you leave your friends so abruptly?"

Mrs. Asher sighed. "Between ourselves, I was suffering severely from a complication of complaints. My doctor forced me—quite *forced* me to break off all my gayeties, and to seek refuge in a quiet retreat."

"Where was it? In the mountains?" asked Mrs. de Trow, with evidence of a keen curiosity.

"No, not exactly in the mountains," replied Mrs. Asher, as she remembered certain wide and uninteresting reaches of prairie about this same retreat, "but there were very high, very high——" She was going to say buildings, but changed it in time to "rocks."

"Very high rocks — why, how odd!" replied Mrs. de Trow, "with beautiful expanses of country, though—fine views and all that——"

Mrs. Asher interrupted her. "Oh, pray let us drop that place. Its only recommendation is that it has cured me. Let us rather talk about the absent ones: that dear Princess de Xamarinda and little Lord Summerset de Vere. Does his mother-in-law still worry him as of old, and is it true, quite true, that Mme. de Xama-

rinda could not invite her mother to meet
the Prince?"

"Perhaps you would like to hear about
the Vicomte de Dindon?" said Mrs. de
Trow pointedly.

"Ah, yes! I was quite forgetting him.
Do tell me about that picturesque young
man."

"They say he took your departure much
to heart," said Mrs. de Trow. "Became
romantic, adopted the grand, gloomy, and
peculiar style; but, you know, he was
always so very foolish."

Mrs. de Trow made it an invariable prac-
tice never to turn the cold shoulder upon
people so long as they were above the
ground—a course that was as praiseworthy
from prudential considerations, as it was
charitable from a Christian standpoint.
Yet, as it would seem from the foregoing
conversation, she failed to receive her
friend with her usual *empressement.* A
glance at Mrs. de Trow's position may
throw light on her behavior. She had
brought Maracovini and the English diplomat from Paris with her; a narrow-chested

little Spaniard named Pepino had been picked up in Rome as a possible substitute for M. de Maracovini (should that gentleman's pride at any moment break down, and he carry himself away to pastures new); while a good-looking young Turk engaged in a mercantile house here, and not yet accustomed to a Yankee woman's foolings, had also been added to her suite. She had them all four safe under her wing; and the appearance of Mrs. Asher upon the scene aroused in her the same lively sensations which the appearance of a hawk in the sky occasions in the mother of a brood of chickens.

XXVIII.

SPURNED BY THE QUIRINAL YOU HAVE STILL THE VATICAN.

Now, when the court ball took place, all the Americans present, with one solitary exception, were received with marked favor by the queen. That exception was Mrs. Asher.

Next morning the clerical papers found an excuse for this in her well-known Catholic sentiments, and in her large gifts, while in Paris, to the Church. In point of fact, she had not given a single sou to any charity, but the reputation of having done so was sufficient to bring a call the same afternoon from a well-known monsignor, who was always on the lookout for possible benefactors of the church.

Spurned by the Quirinal, the lady realized the advantage of gaining the Vatican, and insisted on the visitor's remaining to dinner; for, as it happened, the servants were laying the cloth for that meal in the next room. To this proposal he acquiesced with promptness, and a true catholicity of sentiment; since she informed him that the American ambassador to France and his wife, who were not of his Church, were also to be of the party.

Mr. Jackson happened to be in great good spirits that evening, and he struck up an immediate friendship with the prelate; but Mrs. Jackson looked at the guest with less favor. His priestly garb, his good humor, and his stories grated on her; while his appreciation of the Chianti wine, indifferent as it was, seemed unbecoming in a prelate of any denomination. Combined with her graciousness, there was sometimes manifest in Mrs. Jackson a certain little primness, as I have said; therefore, as a sort of moral disclaimer, she found occasion to allude—very delicately, to be sure, but still to allude—to her missionary pursuits, and to the good work the Methodists were doing in the cause of total abstinence in Dianapolis.

"Ah! then it is in Greece that madame resides," exclaimed the monsignor, in evident perplexity.

"In Greece," cried the lady. "Oh, no, sir! Dianapolis is the capital of——"

"Those who live out of it irreverently designate it as the Hoosier State," said the judge, coming to his wife's rescue.

"Ah! I see," cried the monsignor, recognizing the spirit rather than the point of the remark. Then turning to Mrs. Asher—"but this dear Signor Jacqueson is a veritable *farceur*."

Monsignor also had that highest art (born of quick sympathy) of adapting his conversation to all hearers; and, finding that his previous line was not appreciated by the elder lady, he went on to speak of his experience in heathen lands, dwelling on the hardships and dangers he had encountered. As Mrs. Jackson listened, she began to grow reconciled to his dress and unctuous manner, while the fat, priestly face (mottled to the verge of apoplexy by enjoyment of the dinner) came to have a certain pathos. Before the guest departed, he had actually secured her consent to accompany Mrs. Asher to a private interview with His Holiness which he promised to arrange for them in the near future.

XXIX.

NEXT day, with her usual kindness, Mrs. Jackson suggested that the dentist and his wife should also be included in this party. The dentist and his wife expressed a desire to take certain friends, whose acquaintance they had made at the *table d'hôte*. The consequence was that the list swelled to dimensions which required a postponement to one of the regular days of public reception.

Mrs. Asher was extremely annoyed. To be lumped in with a mob of dentists, chance hotel acquaintances, and the like was intolerable; so she cast about for some means of showing to the Lovejoys her exclusiveness, in such a way that the Jacksons could not take umbrage at it.

"I'm getting up an expedition to Tivoli," she found occasion to observe to Mr. Jackson, before the dentist's wife. "I have so many friends that I must strictly limit

the number to ten.   Of course, I expect you
and Mrs. Jackson."

Mr. Jackson's loyal nature evinced itself
in a paternal desire to show by his own
conduct his disapproval of the derogatory
reports concerning Mrs. Asher, some of
which had reached his ear.

"Certainly, my dear, we'll go with pleasure," he replied.

The sole hesitation of Mrs. de Trow in
as readily promising to attend was on the
score of her flock; but a constitutional
antipathy to being left out of any kind of
festivity, be it a fancy ball or a prayer
meeting, tempted her to brave the risk; so
she went, taking with her the Englishman,
the Sardinian, the Spaniard, and the Turk.

Mrs. Jackson, finding herself fatigued
by a conscientious course of sight-seeing,
begged at the last moment to be excused,
leaving Mr. Jackson to represent them
both.

By an accident, quite natural to hired
conveyances, one of the carriages on the
return from this expedition was compelled
to stop on the road for repairs.   As all the

seats in the remainder were occupied, and the rest of the party had engagements in the city to dine, Mrs. Asher and Mr. Jackson insisted on becoming the sole victims of the mishap, by waiting for the rehabilitation of the vehicle. Thus they arrived in Rome an hour or so behind their friends. The circumstances would have passed unnoticed by Mrs. Jackson, but for the fussiness of Mrs. de Trow, who had run in to explain to Mrs. Jackson why Mr. Jackson and Mrs. Asher would be late. Nothing was further from Mrs. de Trow's intentions than to wound or to arouse suspicion in the wife's breast; but Mrs. de Trow occasionally allowed her tongue to carry her away. Having developed a pronounced friendship for Mrs. Asher, her feminine instincts could not avoid a little dig at that lady, particularly as her fears concerning her flock had been half realized, Mrs. Asher having shown a dangerous tendency to "swoop" during the earlier portion of the expedition. It was, therefore, natural that she should casually mention some of the stories going the rounds about Mrs. Asher, and incidentally introduce, as a matter of current gossip, the fact that nothing but Mr. Jackson's earnest solicitation had induced the master of ceremonies to admit of her presentation at court.

"I only tell you this to show you how cruel and venomous the world in which we live is," she said lightly; then, having eased her mind as to her friend, she hurried off to dress for dinner.

Mrs. Jackson had heard of the infatuation of men of her husband's age for women of Mrs. Asher's. Besides, she had never quite appreciated the sense of leaving Paris and coming to Rome. Could the arguments of her husband have been adopted as a mere pretext to renew his acquaintance with this woman? It was too ridiculous for contemplation. Yet she resolved to watch Mrs. Asher very quietly —which she did; and she also resolved to cease worrying about the incident—a resolution which, being a woman, she did not keep. In other words, she was in a condition that would make her view the most ordinary circumstance as suspicious.

Such an one occurred in connection with this very audience with the Pope.

"Do you know," Mrs. Asher observed a few days later to Mr. Jackson, speaking in his wife's presence, "do you know sometimes I think that you had better not go to this interview after all."

"And why not, my dear?" inquired the judge.

"Well, you are accredited to a government that is especially jealous of the Vatican; and it might, in some wise, complicate matters for you when you return to your post. I am not aware whether there is any value in my suggestion, but I thought it well to mention it to you, for I feel myself responsible for introducing to you the monsignor."

"I see your argument, my dear; while I consider myself merely a tourist, without official responsibilities in Italy, it might on the whole be better not to go—or at least to postpone the audience till I can have time to consider the question. Why did that objection never strike you, mother?" he pleasantly turned to his wife and inquired.

"But if we do not go," urged Mrs. Jackson, "it may cause remark: our names have been already sent in."

"No, they have not been sent in yet," said Mrs. Asher; "and, even if they were, I could arrange it with the monsignor."

Mrs. Jackson turned coldly away, but she could logically urge no further objection. Mrs. Asher's arguments seemed well taken; and, moreover, she had already expressed hesitation herself at kneeling before the Pope. In fact, it was only when her husband reminded her that Protestants of all denominations went, and that she must not set herself above others, that these scruples had been stilled. Yet, to have him withdraw at Mrs. Asher's suggestion did not improve matters. It seemed to show the influence this woman had secured over him.

They had been invited to a grand review this same afternoon; but neither the lovely drive to the grounds, nor the wide, spreading plain, nor all the brilliant troops that filed and counterfiled past them, could lighten the heavy weight in Mrs. Jackson's breast.   No, nor the marked consideration which they received from royalty—for his majesty, dismounting from his charger, accompanied the ambassador on foot to the reviewing point; while Mrs. Jackson was invited to come and sit with the queen in her own carriage.

XXX.

"OH, where is he, where is he? You know he is the only husband I have."

It is Mrs. de Trow's voice, and she wrings her hands, and looks disconsolately about the honey-combed ruins of Cæsar's palace, on the highest elevation of which she happens to be standing. Mrs. de Trow had developed the curious propensity of losing her husband on every possible occasion; not so much through any fault of his own, poor man, as because of the speed with which that worldly-minded lady was wont to scamper through the most sacred or profane place of interest. Thus, wherever they go together, Mr. de Trow is sure to be left behind in some dark nook or crevice. Whereupon, the Englishman, the Spaniard, the Sardinian, and the Turk are thrown into spasms of disquietude, as to whose task it shall be to return and fish him back to the light of day.

On the present occasion, he had been abandoned in one of the half-ruined chambers whose arched roofs forming, as it were, a series of imperfect terraces, constitute the stupendous plateau known as Cæsar's Palace. Mr. de Trow emerging into view, the lady's grief subsided; and, reseating herself, she resumed her interrupted conversation. This was not inspired by the glorious if decaying remnants of art that were about her; nor by the majestic ruins which lay grouped around the Forum in the plain below her; nor by the Appian Way, though each of its great flat paving stones could be distinctly discerned from where she sat. She was merely speaking about Mrs. Asher—which was a trifle indiscreet, since that lady was barely a biscuit's throw distant, with three of the quartette.

Possibly her detachment of so unfair a proportion of the flock from their rightful owner inspired the animus of what Mrs. de Trow was saying to the Englishman, who alone remained by her side.

"Of course, I would not hint at anything wrong, but it looks very much as if there was something she desired to conceal, otherwise, why should she absent herself so mysteriously? Every effort of mine to discover where she has been has failed. Then, there was all the talk about the vicomte's debts. Of course, it is an old story now, and I never believed it; but, you must confess, it did look odd—her leaving Paris so soon after. There is something sinister, uncanny about it all. Do you know what I think she is?" and Mrs. de Trow paused to give effectiveness to her denunciation. "I think she is a vampire— nothing more or less."

"Ah! there you are, my dear," she continued, as Mrs. Asher herself approached. "I was just pointing out to this unappreciative Englishman the meaning of life in prehistoric times. How I should have liked to live in those days—in the days of Cæsar, Trojan, Romulus, and Doremus. Think how they struggled and died; perhaps in that very arena (pointing to the Colosseum with her red sunshade), only to make a Roman holiday, as Milton has it,"

"Ah, yes! in Rome one dreams," exclaimed Signor de Maracovini pensively.

"One dreams of Paris cooking—now confess you do," said the Englishman. "At least, that's all I've dreamt of. Haven't had what they call in the States a square meal since I've been here. But misfortunes never cease. Whv if 'Knock-me-down-with-a feather' hasn't played hookey again."

It was a false alarm. Mr. de Trow had merely seated himself behind the base of a broken column, from which he was contemplating the scene of departed empire beneath him.

"You have no romance in your soul," said Mrs. de Trow, looking severely at the Britisher. "If my poor dear husband had disappeared again, it would have been you I should have sent after him as a punishment."

"As a punishment to whom?" asked Mrs. Asher; "to the errant husband, to us, or to himself?"

"To all round," said the Britisher; and they all laughed (exactly why I do not know) except the Turk, who looked glum.

Mrs. Asher instinctively felt that Mrs. de Trow had been talking about her. The next remark of Mrs. de Trow gave her the opportunity of squaring the account.

"To tell you the truth," continued Mrs. de Trow, still alluding to the English diplomat, "he regrets being down here at all, and spending a vacation away from the hunting field. What can you do with such a man?"

"Why not occasionally humor him?" said Mrs. Asher, brightly. "I have an idea that I think will be agreeable 'all round,' as he says."

"What is it—what is it?" was inquired as with one voice.

"Why, that we try a day with the hounds. I long for a dash across country. Do you not also, my dear?" and she turned to Mrs. de Trow.

The account was squared by the mere suggestion of the different pictures the two women would present on horseback.

"But I have no habit," pleaded Mrs. de Trow.

"I will lend you one of mine—I have two."

The idea of Mrs. de Trow in Mrs. Asher's habit was even more than Mrs. de Trow's flock could stand. The Englishman burst into a hearty laugh; Maracovini and the little Spaniard looked sympathetic, and the Turk looked sad, which is the way in which the Orientals evince their appreciation of humor.

"I will confine myself to my carriage," said Mrs. de Trow with dignity. "I have never approved of women dashing across country, as you call it." She saw now what her friend was driving at.

"How charming that will be," went on Mrs. Asher. "You will follow us to pick up the wounded;" then, turning to the Sardinian—"under such circumstances I am sure Signor de Maracovini will ride."

Signor de Maracovini grinned, though his heart fell. His gallantry could not refuse any task imposed by a beautiful woman, while Pepino and the Turk were burning for any means to distinguish themselves in the eyes of their fair charmer.

Though nothing more was said at the time, Mrs. Asher did not let the matter drop; and, when a day or so later the carriages of the two friends drew together on the Pincian, she recurred to it, insisting that the Englishman should secure mounts for the whole party, with the exception of Mrs. de Trow, who could not, of course, be induced to reconsider her decision.

XXXI

MR. PETTIGREW AT LAST GAINS A CLUE.

"Monsieur Antel."

"Voilà, Monsieur le Charge d'Affaires!" and the chief clerk stands erect before Mr. Pettigrew; for, intimate though he was with Mr. Pettigrew, he accorded the same strict deference to his superiors which he rigidly required from the inferior clerks to himself.

"Do you remember telling me some time back last summer of a visitor who called to inquire about Mrs. Asher at the embassy? It was one day during the absence of Mr. Jackson and myself."

"*Parbleu*, monsieur—he was not easily forgotten."

"Will you have the goodness to describe him again?"

"Well, I should say he was near fifty years of age; and, though tall, a back deeply bent as by study or by sorrow. He had a long black grayish beard—and his face had that livid hue of the worker in a lead mine. In short, it was a head that one might expect to see in some picture of the Resurrection by Doré—as of a new life breathed into the decay of death, and shining through the sockets. Monsieur le Chargé, those eyes burnt into my very soul."

"Have you any idea, why he was seeking Mrs. Asher?" asked Mr. Pettigrew.

"Except they be tradesmen, men seek women generally but for two considerations—love or hate."

"You seem to be a philosopher; but which of these emotions do you think influenced this man?"

"There, monsieur, you ask me too much. I will only guarantee my reputation that it had nothing to do with the collection of any bill, save it be a draft against the past."

"You have never seen him since?"

"Never; and, to tell you the truth, I am not particularly anxious to do so."

"Antel," said Mr. Pettigrew, "you may order me a cab."

As the door closed on the chief clerk, he laid his finger on the side of his nose. " When M. le Secrétaire calls for a cab at this hour of the morning, something decidedly important must be *sur le tapis.*"

M. Antel's inference was quite correct. After prolonged correspondence between his friend in Dianapolis and the consul in Cairo, Mr. Pettigrew had been supplied with many particulars concerning Mrs. Asher's career; but it was only to-day that certain further details reached him, making the chain of evidence complete. These largely concerned her marriage; and, on reading them over, M. Antel's visitor assumed strange possibilities. The secretary keenly regretted, therefore, that he had not paid more attention to the chief clerk when he had originally reported the visit to him; and his purpose in ordering a cab was to try and learn through the police whether the man could be still in Paris.

If you can give an accurate description to the authorities, you can obtain information concerning anyone who has been in the city for ten years back. The member of an embassy is accorded especial facilities in such matters ; so, in less than an hour's time, Mr. Pettigrew learned that such a personage as he depicted had actually arrived in Paris on the morning of the 15th of June, and had taken up his quarters in a small lodging house in the neighborhood of Belleville. In the reports which landlords are obliged to make of their guests to the police, the man figured under the name of Horton—his birthplace and last residence being vaguely put down as America. He was stated to have picked up a precarious livelihood during the period of his residence in the city by playing in the orchestras of second-rate theaters. On the 10th of December he had left Paris for parts unknown. As this was but the 19th of December, Mr. Pettigrew had only missed him by nine days. It was very provoking ; but why had he remained so long in Paris, and whither had he gone? If this was really Mrs. Asher's husband, the difference in name could be readily accounted for by a desire to avoid notice. Further, the date of his arrival in Paris—

namely, June 15—coincided with Mrs. Asher's departure to Dianapolis, and might explain the abruptness of her movements.

With the hope of learning more, Mr. Pettigrew next drove to the lodging house mentioned by the police. He found the landlord somewhat reluctant to answer questions, but the glitter of a ten-franc piece won his confidence, and he admitted remembering his lodger perfectly well. His description tallied with that of all the others. The lodger was a sad, odd-looking man, speaking little French, but a great musician, supporting himself by playing in the orchestras of theaters, or in *cafés chantants*, on the violin, and sometimes on the piano. In fact, he played all instruments equally well, though he was continually losing his place, because of a very odd peculiarity. It would seem that after playing a few nights intelligently and giving the managers every satisfaction, his thoughts would begin to wander; and his music, leaving the track, so to speak, would evince the mental disturbance he was suffering.

The announcement made a deep impression on Mr. Pettigrew.

"Yes, a great musician, but evidently possessed of one fixed idea," went on the landlord.

"What was that fixed idea?"

The landlord shrugged his shoulders. "Probably in some wise connected with a woman. He passed much of his time in wandering about the streets as if in search of someone."

Had the landlord any idea of the reason of his departure?

"It might be that he had grown tired of waiting whom he sought in Paris, and was resolved to try somewhere else."

Had the landlord any idea of his destination?

"None whatsoever. Ah! perhaps his son would know. The man used to talk more unreservedly to him—made quite a friend of him; and, in odd moments, tried to teach him English. The boy was engaged at *M'sieu Georges' remise.* He earned ten sous a day for carrying the pails to the drivers when they washed their carriages. If monsieur would wait, he would call him. The *remise* was just around the corner."

Mr. Pettigrew signified his willingness to wait; and, after a few minutes, the man returned with his son. No, the boy knew nothing of whither the stranger had gone, nor had he taught him much English. He —the boy—was rather afraid of the man, and had been guyed by his companions for his odd acquaintance. There was only one thing that impressed itself on his recollection, which he had forgotten until this moment: namely, a little slip of paper containing an address, whither, in case any letter came, it should be redirected and forwarded. This piece of paper, the boy, after much fishing, exhumed from an interior pocket— "H. C. Horton, care of American Consul, Cairo, Egypt," was written on the paper.

" Your son has proved the postscript of a young woman's letter," said Mr. Pettigrew enigmatically.

"I do not understand," replied the innkeeper.

"Never mind," answered Mr. Pettigrew —"I do."

Immediately on his return home Mr. Pettigrew wrote a long letter to Mr. Jackson. Never did he find a missive harder to indite. Though he had kept his disappointment in connection with Mrs. Asher to himself, her disappearance had caused him a rude shock. Moreover Mr. Pettigrew was a gentleman and his detective work had been little to his taste, but being possessed of certain particulars it was only right that Mr. Jackson should be informed of them, and he sent him a detailed history of Mrs. Asher's career from its inception. But, regardless of fate, that pretty woman has been preparing to enact the part of Diana ; and this digression as to Mr. Pettigrew's discoveries has enabled her to complete her arrangements.

XXXII.

THERE has always seemed to me some·
thing peculiarly incongruous about fox·
hunting in Rome: the ideas inspired by the
Eternal City and sport being the very
antipodes of each other. Yet, the fields of
the Campagna are broad, the fences high,
and the foxes both numerous and lively.
Therefore, you can have a magnificent gal·
lop, with the only drawback of occasional
stumbling into an overgrown atrium, or of
blundering through the crust of some inno·
cent looking mound, and of being shot with
a mass of rubbish into the long disused
dining room of some suburban villa.

The meet was a little way outside the
Porta Pia, and was one of the most bril·
liant of the season.

Mrs. Asher started with the rest of the
riders when the hounds threw off—grad·
ually attracting attention to herself as one
field after another was passed, and her

superb horsemanship had the chance to make itself manifest. With a light-limbed, wiry steed that jumped like a deer, she was soon leading the field; the large Englishman sailing serenely just behind her, Maracovini (comical in his misery on a large rawboned horse of which he was as much in horror as of the fences) and little Pepino, the Spaniard, following with the Turk in the rear.

Mrs. de Trow and her husband followed in a cabriolet, and in a very bad humor; Mrs. de Trow paying the penalty of her little indiscretion—Mr. de Trow paying the penalty of having expressed the desire of doing something else, and consequently being compelled, poor man, to accompany madame.

But what is of far more consequence than the above is that following Mr. and Mrs. de Trow came Mr. Jackson in a large landau. Mr. Jackson had not seen Mrs. Asher for several days past. He had been much entertained in official circles, yet his soul craved other association; so with the excuse of hearing how Mrs. Asher had been lately passing her time, he had descended on the morning of the hunt to her sitting room, only to find her on the point of starting forth.

Now Mrs. Asher's pleasure at seeing him was so evident, and her entreaties that he accompany her in her carriage to the meet so sincere, that he entirely forgot a partial agreement he had made to conduct his wife to an open air lecture. Thus he had gone, sad as the admission must be. In the meanwhile, Mrs. Jackson waited. She was one of those women who, when they feel strongly, feel silently. Why did he not come ? she asked herself. She would be late for the lecture, which was one of a course the distinguished antiquarian Lanciani was giving on the House of the Vestals. The lectures were held on the very site of its ruins ; and to miss one now was to break the continuity. These lectures were the only thing in Rome she had unaffectedly enjoyed ; for, though by no means unappreciative of the wonders of the ancient city, its gloom chilled her. It was intensely disappointing that he did not come. But the hours rolled on, and with them the gloom of the great city increased.

In point of fact, Mrs. Asher had not expected Mr. Jackson to go with her farther than to the meet; the understanding being that the carriage should then return with him to the city, and come back for her at a certain hour, and at an indicated spot. But Mr. Jackson had never seen a pack of hounds throw off before, and the unusual brilliancy of the affair, the bright weather, and the glorious Campagna with its scattered ruins, all fascinated him and drew him on. Thus he continued, keeping in sight of the riders as long as possible, until it became too late for him to return and permit of the carriage meeting Mrs. Asher at the place she had appointed.

It was past five o'clock when they reached the city together, and he stopped in her sitting room for a cup of tea. They were laughing and chatting when Mrs. Jackson entered.

The ambassador noticed nothing unusual in his wife's manner. He had not yet remembered the arrangement he had made with her for the morning, and he proceeded to relate the events of the day for her delectation.   These were certainly harmless enough; but he was in great good spirits, and a trifle excited over the unusual experience.

Mrs. Jackson detected his exhilaration, and it jarred on her.   She had nothing to say against the sport, which he had witnessed, in itself.   It was all very well for young people; but, for a man of his years and position, it seemed undignified, to say the least, while his interest in it appeared but a mark of the frivolity to which, under this woman's influence, he had succumbed.   This secret communion of his with Mrs. Asher, too, that made the wife a mere listener to the incidents of the day, instead of being a participator in its pleasures, added poignancy to her desertion.   And as she stood there it seemed to her her eyes were suddenly opened by his conduct to a condition of affairs that naught but her blindness had concealed before.   A light word from Mrs. Asher fanned the smoldering embers into flame.

"I hope you are not jealous of my robbing you of him the entire day," she smiled.

Mrs. Jackson drew herself up to her full height. "No, madam; I am not prone to be jealous of one like yourself, however substantial may be the grounds you afford me for being so."

"Why, madam, what do you mean?" exclaimed the judge, surprised at the reception his recital had met with.

"But I must insist," continued the lady, "that, as my own dignity is concerned, you shall respect his; and that in future your appointments may be kept in a less conspicuous manner than they were to-day."

Mrs. Asher looked up in astonishment.

"Why, madam, are you crazy? I must ask you to restrain yourself," said Mr. Jackson.

"No, sir; I am not crazy; though I should think that I might well put that same question to you;" and the irate woman turned and faced her husband. "When I see you throwing yourself away upon an adventuress, whose only object is to secure

her own social advancement through your
official position ; when I see you unblush-
ingly flaunting her in the face of the world
—though the world has already turned its
back upon her—then I may well infer you
have lost your senses, and that your appreciation of the world's good opinion has
been blunted by your intrigue."

Mr. Jackson was seriously embarrassed.
Because Mrs. Asher was unprotected—
because she was criticised—was the very
reason why he should champion her; not to
have offered her his support would have
been repugnant to his manhood; besides,
the first duty of his official position was
to protect the oppressed. That his wife
should take another view of his relations
with Mrs. Asher surprised him inordinately; and, for a moment, he believed
his wife was beside herself.

Mrs. Asher looked at her with a grand
air of pitying disdain, and swept out of the
room.

.   .   .   .   .

Three hours later Mrs. Asher was in
her sitting room, when Mr. Jackson was

announced. His manner was extremely embarrassed and she saw at a glance that he resented his wife's harshness. The fact is a man can never view these matters quite in the same light as his better half. Mrs. Asher listened to his excuses without reply. She had been deeply, mortally offended. While not a good woman, she was not entirely a bad one, and the insinuations of the wife were less than half true. She had clung to Mr. Jackson not alone for social advancement, but because he was strong and loyal. And as he talked on, the future opened before her in all its desolation; suddenly an idea, wild and extravagant, but bred of her despair, occurred to her. Might she not detach him from his wife to herself? Once under her influence, the divorce courts could sanction the rest. Such unions had happened before —why not again? The idea strangely suited her present mood. She let her head fall into her clasped hands, and presently Mr. Jackson heard her sobs.

"Oh, you must restrain yourself, my dear, you must restrain yourself!" he urged.

She lifted her eyes and looked at him fixedly. "You do not realize how a woman, situated as I am, alone in the world and with no one to protect her, feels such accusations."

"I know, I know," exclaimed Mr. Jackson contritely.

"And yet," she continued, "if I thought you had any such feeling for me as your wife implied I would not mind."

"I do not quite catch your meaning," said Mr. Jackson.

"I mean I realize that you only care for me as a friend, if you care for me at all."

"And how else would you have me care for you?"

"Can't you tell?"

Mr. Jackson surveyed her with an astonishment no language can express.

"Say that you will not desert me," she continued. "My life has been so hard, I have had so much to struggle against, you will not be hard too."

"You mean to imply, madame, that you actually care for me?" he inquired at length.

"Can I help caring for you after all the

kindness you have shown me? When I think of it all and realize that it must cease, I—I—" and she sank back on the lounge in a paroxysm of tears.

"But what would you have me do?"

Mrs. Asher's time had come, all else had been preliminary; she rose to her feet and approached him. "I would have you re-fuse to discard me at any one's instance, I would have you tell me that you would make any sacrifice for my sake, I would have you tell me—tell me, in short, what a woman who cares for a man wants to hear from his lips. My whole future is in your hands."

Mr. Jackson dimly recognized what her words implied, but he believed her sincere and he was moreover deeply moved. He began to say something, but hesitated and faltered, when suddenly catching sight of himself in a mirror, of his gray hairs and his wrinkles he broke away from her and left the room.

Mrs. Asher's tears subsided. He had not protested, he would return. The first trick was hers and the cards had been forced upon her, but— Ah, well! the world was now her foe and she must conquer.

Mr. Jackson went out into the street. He wanted air, and he wanted to think. No, no, he had not protested as he should, and he recognized his own turpitude. The twilight had just deepened into evening, and already the firmament was bright with stars. And as he went two pictures kept recurring to him: one of a life poetic and roseate and perfumed, through which the soft strains of enticing music seemed to float—the other a picture of his actual life, a life of Congressional Records, of dry statistics, and of routine. Why could not society, nay, morality, reconcile and permit the realization of the two pictures—the life of music and of poesy with that of the homely virtues? The classic civilizations admitted of both, when Aspasia was recognized, and honored. The very chivalry of his nature drew him to this woman, and the recent severity of his wife toward her accentuated his feelings. We never know the depths of our nature till they are sounded, and in us all are depths that no plumb can reach when woman holds the line.

He was highly wrought up, as only that man who has never known temptation, and to whom it is presented without warning, can be. As he went he resented his years, that seemed to render his position grotesque, and especially the livery of gray in which time decks its slaves. And through his troubled thoughts sprang up a secret resentment against nature, that for pain and sorrow finds no compensation, yet for every pleasure an antidote, making sickness and disease, instead of health, contagious, and then expects man to regard her as a mother.

The streets he had followed became narrower and less frequented; and, suddenly passing under a ponderous arch, he found himself on the border of the Campagna.

By the route by which he had come, the transition between the town and country was abrupt. Save for the barking of a dog, the tinkling of a mule bell, or the lowing of distant cattle, all was as still as the stars above his head. Here and there along the road before him were crumbling mounds, tombs of great men of imperial Rome. How vain they proved human effort to be! How ridiculous the struggle for distinction, and how true that greatest truth: "Dust thou art, and unto dust thou shalt return."

The life of the senses at least had this advantage; it brought enjoyment while it lasted, which ambition never did. Again the memory of what he had read of classic times came back to him—the times of Aspasia and when the state was more important than the family. But Rome had absorbed its civilization, its art and its religion from Greece, and what had become of Rome? Destroyed—wiped out—leaving naught but a heap of ruins. As he stood there beneath the stars, amid the long lines of tombs, the great secret of nations was revealed to him. Because of these Aspasias first Greece and then Rome fell. Aye! and to his distorted imagination a greater lesson seemed revealed to him—a lesson of nature, viz., that as life comes through woman, so through woman comes destruction; and, by a sort of retributive justice, in pursuance of that inexplicable wave-like principle on which the universe moves, woman makes man and, in the end, all civilization, suffer for the torments to which she has been subjected in bringing man into existence. A reflection so unusual to his ordinary trend of thought startled him.

He returned to his hotel wearied and disturbed. He knew that she was in the hotel, and the temptation was keen to go to her, and let the nations depend for their strength on other and more general foundations. In this mood he sat down in the reading room; and, as he sat there, he remembered a letter marked confidential, from Mr. Pettigrew, which he had not yet read. He listlessly broke the seal.

"My dear Judge," it began, "I think you will do me the credit of appreciating that any communication to you of a painful nature is an extremely distasteful task; and yet I should feel that I had ill requited the many kindnesses received at your hands, did I withhold any information which

I think you have a right to hear. That
this will shatter your confidence in one who
enjoys the distinguished privilege of your
own and Mrs. Jackson s friendship cannot
blind me to my sense of duty."

The Judge skipped an intervening page
of explanations as to how certain particulars
had reached Mr. Pettigrew, and he resumed
at these lines: "I refer to a lady you have
known by the name of Mrs. Asher. I give
you her history in its proper order. Con-
cisely stated, she is the daughter of the
keeper of a small tavern, the proximity of
which to West Point brought her into frequent contact with an officer stationed at
that military post. An engagement re-
sulted, which, through the interference of
the suitor's friends, was broken off. In
pique at her treatment, she gave heed to
the importunities of a man considerably
her senior in years, who, from the time she
was a girl at the academy where he taught
music, had persisted in his attentions to
her.

"The union proved ill-advised. Though
born in America, her husband was of Ger-

man parentage; and, being of a morose, suspicious nature, proved little inclined to make allowances for the difference in their age. In fact, it is doubtful whether his mind was not slightly unbalanced. People said he chafed at the limited horizon of his professional prospects, and he was thought to brood over the failure of an opera, to the construction of which he had devoted the best ten years of his life. Under these circumstances, she turned for consolation to her former lover; and one of their stolen interviews coming to the ears of her husband, his jealousy transcended all bounds, and, with threats and upbraidings, he drove her from his house.

"People in the neighborhood remember the circumstance well, from the indecorous manner in which it was revealed to them. In addition to teaching music, he was employed as organist in one of the principal churches of the village where the school was situated; and, on the morning succeeding the rupture, he took his usual place (for it was Sunday) in the choir. I quote from one of the local papers.

"'For a time nothing odd was noticed in the performance; but, when the collection was being taken, the voluntary began to assume strange variations; flashes of weird and unwonted sound darted like summer lightning through the solemn rhythm, to be succeeded by snatches of dances that were as inopportune as they were profane. Never were such strains heard in a church before; when, at last, one connected melody predominating, the opera, that had so long slumbered in the disordered brain, was poured out in a maddened torrent.

"'It was not till the music had ceased that an effort was made to dislodge him. The sexton and a deacon, who mounted to the gallery for that purpose, found him sitting with his head buried in his hands. At their approach, he woke as from a dream; and, shaking himself free from their grasp, advanced to the front of the gallery, and made the startling announcement to the congregation that his troubles had temporarily affected his mind. Then, with an utterance as impassioned as his music, he told his domestic miseries. "His charges," continued Mr. Pettigrew, "however ill-timed and possibly exaggerated, roused public sentiment against Captain Asher, and the too evident derangement which inspired them was laid at his door. Effort was made to hush the matter up, but he was finally compelled to resign his commission. In the meanwhile the discarded wife had procured a divorce, and turning his thoughts to foreign service the captain induced her to marry him and to accompany him to Egypt, whose ruler at that time was engaged in the reconstruction of his army. Here he succeeded in procuring employment as instructor of riding to a cavalry regiment under the command of a relative of the Khedive.

"This occupation proved little to his taste and so successfully did he cultivate the friendship of his superior that he eventually secured a concession from the Government in connection with a gambling establishment at Port Said. Some aver his emoluments excited the envy of the Government—others that he so far forgot what was due his patron as to include him among the victims at his tables. At all events, the enterprising officer was found one morning in bed in a condition of coma from which he never rallied, and Mrs. Asher repaired to Paris to enjoy the fruits of her prudence in having persuaded him to invest his very considerable profits in French rents and under her own name. Here in some way she learned that her divorce had been defective, and consequently her marriage to Captain Asher was void. "I now come to inference," continued Mr. Pettigrew, "she certainly went to Diana-polis to perfect her divorce, but I infer the necessity of this step was created by the reappearance of her husband. Probably he had heard through the press of her being here, and it revived his animosity against her. Owing to the secrecy of her movements he failed to learn where she had gone; and, up to within a few days, had simply stayed on in Paris in hopes of her return. Then he had proba-bly repaired to Cairo on the slender chance of finding her there—failing to hear, in the meantime, that she had reappeared in Rome."

In confirmation of these surmises, Mr. Pettigrew recalled to the judge's memory the strange visitor who in the summer had stopped at the embassy to inquire about Mrs. Asher—recited the particulars he, Mr. Pettigrew, had learned of this person's life while residing in Paris—recited the many points of similarity he possessed in common with Mrs. Asher's husband, and gave, as a proof of the belief that he had subsequently gone to Cairo, the address produced by the hotel-keeper's son for the forwarding of letters.

Mr. Pettigrew closed his epistle with the unanswerable statement that, while his belief as to her pursuit by an aggrieved husband might be groundless, there was enough known and proved about the lady to make her anything but a desirable associate for Mrs. Jackson.

.   .   .   .

Never was a missive better timed. It completely changed the current of Mr. Jackson's thoughts. As he read his intoxication evaporated; and, at the close of the letter, he was once more himself. Though some instinct told him that the main lines of the story were true, yet he felt that he ought not to accept them unanswered. He called a servant, and begged to learn whether Mrs. Asher would receive him. Ten minutes later he was again in her sitting room, and placed the letter before her.

She read it attentively, then threw it aside. "Suppose it were true, would you consider me past redemption?" she inquired.

"I shall always believe that you have been more sinned against than sinning; but, under the circumstances, I deem it advisable that our intercourse should cease."

"Then the world is nothing to me."

"Madam, you have been trying to make a fool of me."

"Never; I would give up my life for you," she replied.

The false note was now quite distinct.

"My dear young woman ," he briefly answered, "though you may not believe it, I have had a pretty wide experience of life, and I have learned this: that a woman never gives up anything for a man past fifty, except the debt be paid at usurious interest."

Mrs. Asher drew away from him. "Then you can go," she said curtly; "if that is your belief, I can save myself the trouble of any further conversation. I would be alone." And he went without another word.

Mrs. Asher read the whole situation at a glance. Even should Mr. Jackson keep to himself the information he now possessed, their relations could never be the same; and without his support she recognized herself on the eve of social collapse. Marriage now alone could save her. Her hope concerning the ambassador had been too extravagant, but the vicomte was left. Seizing a telegraph blank, she hurriedly wrote that she would be at Nice by a certain date, begging him to meet her at an address which she gave. The next evening she departed; and, by a curious coincidence, Signor de Maracovini followed by a later train, his pride having at last consented to break with Mrs. de Trow.

XXXIII.

MARRIAGE AS A LAST RECOURSE FOR THE DESPERATE.

ONCE started, Mrs. Asher's spirits rose with every revolution of the wheel. She had played the *grande dame* till the restraint had become well-nigh intolerable; and, by the time the train that bore her reached the Mediterranean shore, her sense of freedom was complete. All appealed to her mood: the blue sky that descended like a god of old to mingle lover-like with the sea, till all dividing line of horizon was lost; the wavelets that laved the shore and, in coquettish sport, kissed the pebbles on the beach; why, the very rocks that jutted out into the laughing sea appeared *couleur de rose*, and the castles that crowned their crests seemed to smile rather than to frown. All nature held a caress, and the breeze was perfumed as a lover's breath.

How much was lost in that vain struggle for respectability — respectability represented by a Mrs. Jackson. Mrs. Jackson indeed! How she loathed and abominated the combination of qualities of which that estimable lady seemed to her the embodiment. What a contrast too was the brightness here to the gloom of ages that hung over the city she had left. No! life with its pulsations, its instincts, its hopes, its quick joys, and even its woes, for her! Rome like a shadow was behind her, and intoxication before. But she must win the Vicomte and she pictured the impassioned telegram that would be waiting her at Nice, and even began to conjure up a sentiment for the youthful author. He was handsome after all; but why, why, in conscience sake, was he not dark? Brown was the tint for men, as blonde was for women. She argued on the best of all premises, being blonde herself.

Arrived at Nice, she found the following answer to her dispatch: " A thousand regrets. Impossible to come for the moment. I write this evening."

The morning's mail brought the promised explanation, announcing the vicomte's engagement.

Yes, the Vicomte de Dindon was actually engaged to be married. Accustomed as were his friends to associate the unexpected with him, the fact surprised them no less than Mrs. Asher. If we must admit it, too, when he found himself in the meshes, he was as much astonished as any of the rest. It had come about in this wise. His interview with the head of the progressive party had been followed by a long paralysis of mental inactivity. Deeming the occasion favorable for a word of advice, his father came to him one morning, and very abruptly ejaculated: "My son, why do you not marry and settle down?"

A curious characteristic about the vicomte was that, if you wished to win him over, you must take him by storm. If, after considerable argument and preparation, you urged the advantage of a short trip to the coast of England, say, he would hesitate and find better arguments for remaining where he was. If you approached him suddenly, however, and proposed, without giving any reasons, an expedition to an island in the imperfectly discovered lake of Victoria Nyanza, or better still, to the South Pole, to investigate, perhaps, the theory of perpetual motion, he would be seized with sudden enthusiasm and would very likely exclaim: "Why, there is certainly an idea."

Therefore, when his father, who knew his peculiarities, proposed marriage, he did so with a precipitancy that made it attractive, and captured the young man immediately by urging no arguments in its favor. Now, the moment anything struck his fancy, the vicomte himself immediately found good and effective reasons to recommend it—putting, as it were, the logical cart before the horse, and making his arguments subsidiary to his decision instead of basing it on them. In the present case, the pros were so palpable that it surprised him that the idea had never occurred to him before.

The lady whom his father went on to name was rich, and with wealth one could rule the world. She was *brune*, which must mean constancy, since Mrs. Asher was fair; and besides, it would be a graceful way of showing the latter how well he could do without her, should she ever again appear on the surface of fashionable life. Altogether, the suggestion was a good one.

The announcement came upon Mrs. Asher like a mild species of thunderclap. Her control over men had been so absolute that the idea of their independent action was quite outside her calculations. For the first time, she began to experience a faint regard for him. And as the probabilities of marriage receded from her by just so much its value was enhanced. Mrs. Asher was not a vindictive woman—to live and to let live was her object, but she was a desperate woman, and the desperate will strike. How could she break off his engagement? Ah, there was a way, yet would it assist her in her own schemes? Perhaps and perhaps not. But it would remove the first barrier to her ambitions, of this there could be no doubt.

With this barrier removed the rest could be left to chance. Besides, to the least vindictive of us there is a secret pleasure in retaliation. She had nothing to lose now, for she had cut herself off from the world and could at last give rein to her feelings. Yes, she would strike *coute qui coute.*

XXXIV.

THE VISCOUNT'S FALL.

Paris is lying chilled and disconsolate in the icy grasp of a cold winter, albeit a bright, warm day is occasionally interjected as if left over from the autumn, or as a precursor of better days to come in the approaching spring. Then Paris comes to life. Dealers are seen on the Champs-Élysées breaking in four-in-hand teams; gay-looking vehicles emerge like butterflies between showers; military and civilian devotees of sport canter out to the Bois to try their chargers over the well-worn hurdles near the Cercle des Patineurs. But all these indications of outdoor life are spasmodic and exceptional. Paris is indoors; and society, having little to distract its attention, is in an especially favorable mood for making the most of anything in the nature of a scandal. Indeed, there is something atmospheric, I think, behind the susceptibility of the public to receiving and transmitting evil about one of its own members. Certainly, what at one moment will hardly excite an unfavorable remark, at another will be caught up with a species of malign fury, and, leaping from mouth to mouth, will bury the unfortunate subject under a mass of obloquy without giving him so much as a chance to protest. Such proved to be the atmospheric condition of the capital when the news came one morning that the well-nigh forgotten Mrs. Asher had, without any warning, commenced a *procès* against the Vicomte de Dindon for the recovery of twenty-five thousand francs, loaned him seven months ago to pay his gambling debts.

Very likely people had resented the suppression of the story previously, and now found consolation in putting upon it the most serious construction. Besides, what was mere rumor then seemed now established by the suit; and, though having a woman to pay his debts was bad enough, the apparent condition of the arrangement, that this woman should be foisted upon them, gave a sense of personal injury to each. Still again, his engagement to a great heiress had lately raised him into a position of prominence from which his fall would be the more interesting. No light fall did it prove. People refused to look at him in the streets. There were meetings at his club to decide what action ought to be taken; and his *fiancée* grew peevish instead of grandly heroic—the correct attitude for a young woman to assume when her lover is proved worthless. And yet, so far as the suit goes, I think the vicomte was treated very harshly. Mrs. Asher had forced upon him a loan at a moment of great pecuniary embarrassment, and several times, when he had proposed to make arrangements to repay it, she had put him off. Though she had used him as the key to the doors of society he actually believed in her right to enter, and consequently that he was simply introducing to his friends a woman of superlative attractions.

His position became intolerable, for not only his own good name, but his family's, was at stake, nor could any denials on his part remove the entirely erroneous impres-

sion that his parents had been partners to
a nefarious arrangement.

"But it is monstrous—it is monstrous!"
he cried in his despair, as he began to
realize how desperate matters were; and he
wrote an impassioned letter to Mrs. Asher,
commanding her to withdraw her suit.

In ten days, having received no response,
and finding Paris absolutely unendurable,
he resolved to run down to Nice to protest
at her course of action, and further to offer
to pay all that was due her, forgetting that
it was too late to pay, and that it was his
prestige, not money, that was now at stake.

XXXV.

Is there any section of the world so conducive to pleasure as the Riviera, whose head center is Nice, with its palm-lined Promenade des Anglais, its luxurious villas, and its wide stretch of azure sea? If you wish to enjoy yourself riotously, you have Monte Carlo on the one side. If you wish to enjoy yourself sedately, you have Cannes on the other, both bathed in that soft iridescent light that makes of this land one vast Araby the Blest. It is the only locality that I know of where life seems never to be regarded from the standpoint of its painful duties—and as the vicomte glided in the luxurious train along that sunlit shore, he was affected by its glamour and began to regret that his mission was not more in harmony with the surroundings.

He experienced little difficulty in discovering the villa where Mrs. Asher had taken up her abode. As on his first visit eight months before, he was informed that she was at home. Again the same sensuous odor of hothouse flowers assailed him on entering her drawing room, and again she allowed the atmosphere of her *entourage* to work its effects upon him by keeping him waiting.

Much the same surroundings, *mutatis mutandis*, must the old Greek poet have had in his mind when he depicted the home of Circe. Much the same view must he have had in his mind's eye as was to be enjoyed from her windows, and much the same thoughts as those of Circe must have been in the lady's mind when she came in to meet the vicomte.

"Ah! Ulysses has returned," she laughed softly, and she received him as if honor, reputation, the world's opinion were as naught. But the vicomte had come down to protest; and, though the subtle influence of her presence, like some baleful poison, was stealing over him, protest he must.

"But it is nefarious—it is nefarious," he

çried, and he began to pour out the torrent of his wrongs.

She stayed him. "And do you—a man of the world—complain," she asked, "at a woman's pretext to regain one she loves?"

The vanity of the vicomte was his weak point.

"And you love me?" he asked.

The lady sighed as she plucked the petals from a rose. It was at this most inopportune moment that the portières of a side door parted and Signor de Maraco-vini appeared upon the scene. Nothing is more disagreeable than such an interruption. The intruder being without hat or gloves, and coming from the mystery of inner sanctuaries proclaims by his presence domi-ciliary rights that even to an ex-lover is extremely distasteful. Mrs. Asher had carefully planned his entrance.

The vicomte rose and surveyed him with infinite hauteur.

"I will renew this interview, madame, when I can enjoy the privilege of seeing you alone," he said, in his jerky way.

Signor de Maracovini grinned affably,

and then skipped over to the window, where he stood looking out upon the sea and twirling his mustache. Mrs. Asher rose and followed the vicomte to the door. As he was going out, she whispered in her most seductive tones, " Come for me this evening at eight o'clock and take me to dine at the Café Riche ; don't decide now, but write me at the last moment. I will do anything you ask."

XXXVI.

" THE TRUE WOMAN SPEAKS AT LAST."

How extraordinary are the inconsisten-
cies of man where woman is concerned !
Why I have heard of men actually breaking their vows to their wives for other
women's sakes—let alone vows that have
not yet been solemnized by marriage. Not
that the vicomte was going to break
the troth he had so recently plighted—not
he; on the contrary, he had come down
here to confirm it by making this woman
withdraw charges that tended to weaken
his hold upon his *fiancée.* He loved her
—I mean his *fiancée*—he also pitied her
for what she was enduring for his sake.
But what in the name of the devil and the
seven sins gave that Sardinian the run of
Mrs. Asher's house ?   The inconsistency in
this case being that a man who has thrown
over a woman for some other woman's sake,
considers he has still the right to criticise,
if not control, the former's actions.

It was five o'clock, and he wandered disconsolate up and down the Promenade des Anglais, firmly resolved that he would not take her to dine. At last, however, the temptation to speak his mind to her, to show the depth of his contempt and hatred, in fact, to fulfill the purpose of his coming hither, in the execution of which he had been interrupted, proved irresistible; and, as it generally happened with the vicomte when he firmly made up his mind to do or not to do a thing, at the last moment he changed his mind, and did the reverse. So, he wrote that he would meet her at the café she had indicated.

Mrs. Asher proved her thorough knowledge of his character when she insisted upon leaving his decision upon her invitation till the last moment. She also showed her knowledge of human nature when she selected a *tête-à-tête* dinner as the occasion for receiving his reproaches. Just as may be your resentment, firmly resolved as you may be to express it, it is extremely difficult to sit down to table with a beautiful woman and deliberately begin a dispute.

Ordinary courtesy compels you to postpone the attack from one course to another, till there is danger, if the *chef* has done his duty, that the satisfaction of a refined and happy repletion dispels your wrath.

Yes! Mrs. Asher's expedient was a happy one. Besides the original grievance a new source of irritation to the vicomte had arisen, which diverted just so much animus from the complaint he had brought down from Paris. I mean the irritation caused by meeting Signor de Maracovini in her house.

Never did Mrs. Asher exert so much effort to be agreeable, and never did she succeed better. Though the vicomte made several attempts to speak of his two-fold annoyance, she turned him aside like a skillful fencer. It was not till he had left her, and the spell of her charm was broken, that the real enormity of his conduct was realized; then bitter shame—shame for himself—shame for the disgrace he had brought upon his innocent family—assailed him. For people who knew him had seen him dining in her company; and they would infallibly proclaim the fact to the world.

Fate waits like a cat to make her spring successful. Arrived at his hotel, he found a telegram from his father, announcing that his *fiancée* had decided to be no longer bound by her engagement. In less than twenty minutes afterwards, he was waiting in Mrs. Asher's boudoir, having insisted that she receive him, late as was the hour. Then, when she presented herself, he poured upon her head his retarded resentment; and, with the eloquence injustice can alone inspire, showed her the misery she had brought upon him. As she listened, his despair touched some long neglected chord of sympathy. For the first time the completeness of her work was revealed to her. He stood before her disgraced in the sight of men, cast off by the woman he had chosen—chosen only when she herself had deserted him—and responsible before the world for involving his family in the common scandal. All this was her doing, and for what? The attainment of her own selfish and unworthy ends. She could

see, too, that his vanity made his position
the more intolerable.   As he went on, the
force of his protestations struck her with
a kind of a terror; yet there stole upon
her a yearning to make amends.   Falling
on his neck, she confessed the part that she
had played, begging him to go back to his
fiancée and promising to withdraw her suit.
No acting could have attained the same
results, for the true woman spoke out.

Her tears dissolved his anger—his old
passion for her revived.   Never did she
appear more beautiful; she was softened at
last.

"You can only make amends in one way,"
he said.   Then the inconsistency of
the Vicomte reached its apex, but we must
remember that in his case the unexpected
was the only thing to expect.   "You can
marry me."

"Marry you!" she cried, astounded—
"never, never."

"No one else will have me now—you
must."

XXXVII.

THE wedding was arranged for the
morrow and it was the last day of the
carnival at Nice. The city had laid herself out to make it a success; and the
ceremonies, at least so far as the select were
concerned, were to close with a *bal costumè*
in the evening.

All styles and descriptions of dress were
represented on her streets that bright afternoon. There were British admirals sport-
ing with Spanish bull-fighters; clowns in
the most approved attire making eyes at
sober abbesses; monks were flirting with
vivandèires; and devils, catching other
devils by the tails, ceasing their antics for
a moment to throw bouquets at the fair, or
confetti at the unfair (I mean the male)
occupants of the passing carriages.

No carriage in the long array received a

more flattering tribute of flowers than did Mrs. Asher's. But though she had attained her ends a strange pensiveness possessed her. Every now and then she glanced at the figure by her side. Something told her he had already begun to repent. When they returned from their drive she came and put her arms about his neck. "Are you sorry you ever met me?" she asked.

"It might have been better had I not," he replied.

"Then why don't you leave me?" she asked. "Why not go back and renew your engagement? I see you are not happy, to-morrow will be too late."

"In this world there is no going back; we can only advance."

"Don't say that!" she cried. "I would like to feel that I had helped you instead of harming you."

"That would have been impossible for you," he said, and turned brusquely aside.

That conversation remained stamped forever on his memory, and he bitterly recalled in after times his own coldness.

Mrs. Asher hesitated long that evening in arraying herself for the ball; remaining on her balcony, and looking out upon the sea. It was a still, beautiful night. The moon painted the waves with silver, and shed on the town a holy effulgence which, perhaps, it scarcely deserved. Out in the offing the dark hulls of vessels rose dimly above the waters, their lights twinkling and shining like little stars. How many lives, she thought, were to expire in this great universe as those lights would expire before the morning, leaving as little record on the page of time. Her softened mood still lingered from the afternoon.

It was exactly ten o'clock when her maid presented her with a telegram. It broke abruptly upon her meditations. "Just learned that he reached Rome last Wednesday from Cairo. Should he go on to Nice and attempt any molestation, do not hesitate to act. Will come if you advise." It was signed "G. Charteran."

She staggered back and would have fallen but for the railing of the balcony, to which she clung, while a strange, prickling sensation pierced her heart like a thousand needle points. Her maid flew to her side.

"He will interfere with the wedding."

"Who, madame?"

"Read it—read it!" she cried. "All my hopes of quiet, all prospects of happiness gone. Often and often I wake up in the night, and think I see him just as I saw him in Paris. Oh, I shall go mad with it all! I shall get to feel I have no right to live. But we will escape him," she continued, with a sudden change of manner, "for we will fly to-night—anywhere; so long as we escape him."

"But madame really must calm herself. There is no need to fly if madame will only leave everything in my hands. I will notify the police. Madame now has the law on her side. If he really follows madame here, he places himself in the jaws of the lion. They will close upon him; and madame then is free, with all the world before her—youth, beauty, fortune. What more can the heart desire—except it be to have Monsieur le Vicomte as a *mari complaisant!*"

Her thoughts reverted to the vicomte as her gaze again sought the sea. "It sometimes seems a crime to tie him to me."

"And why?"

"I would drag him down to my level. He is so young, so hopeful."

"Madame need have no scruples on that score. These men never think of the level to which they bring our sex."

"I should like to raise him."

"And again, why not? Youth, beauty, fortune, these are the qualities that raise men most in our days. But will not madame now allow me to dress her? It is getting late."

"But, I cannot—I cannot go to the ball with this awful shadow hanging over me. When I remember that——"

"Madame must forget. Recollections are only good for crow's-feet. Come, the eyes of madame are red and inflamed; they must be kept attractive to retain our handsome vicomte. His own may begin to wander, and madame may then miss the last great opportunity to rehabilitate herself before the world."

" Rachel, you are right. I must secure
a recognized position, if only to place myself on a pedestal that raises me above that
man's reach. Now, bring me coffee, strong
and black, and stay, also a drop of brandy.
Aye, yes! *vogue la galere;* 'tis folly to
remember, 'tis wiser to forget."

<h1 style="text-align:center">XXXVIII.</h1>

THE ball was held in one of the large hotels with which Nice is so plentifully provided. It is needless to say that the colony of American exiles mustered in force.

Among the costumes that of the Princess de Xamarinda was the most charming. She represented a good fairy, and with her gold wand, her gauze wings, and her bewitching smile she carried the character off to perfection.

Lady Summerset de Vere represented a young schoolmistress. She looked extremely pretty and prim. A dozen or so of her admirers were her pupils. They were attired in short jackets, huge rolling collars, and short trousers. All had under their arms huge slates, on which they kept writing jests and jibes against each other and their friends. For the |most sedate throw off the yoke of conventionality at an affair of this kind.

Why Mrs. de Trow should have elected to go as Lucrezia Borgia it is hard to say, except that of all conceivable characterizations it was the most unsuited to her. Her husband had taken the same description of liberty with the young Augustus. Possibly, coming so lately from Rome, they deemed that something suggestive of its history in their apparel would be a pretty compliment to the city; though, according to Mrs. de Trow, they had found it after Mrs. Asher's departure "as dull as a scandal about an abstract idea," which of all kinds of scandals is assuredly the dullest.

Our old friend Mrs. O'Hagan personified Diana; and, when we remember her tireless chase of a certain great personage about Europe, we can see an appropriateness in the costume.

Mrs. Asher represented fire. Her dress —a marvel of ingenuity—was slashed upwards, with gleaming tongues of satin flame licking her corsage, and dying away in clouds of blue, smoke-like tulle about her milk-white breast.

The Vicomte de Dindon was in simple Venetian dress, and the darkness of his attire comported with his feelings. As he came into the room Mr. de Trow failed to extend to him his usual effusive welcome, and in his conduct the vicomte read the hopelessness of ever retrieving his position.

For Mr. de Trow was a very thermometer of the social temperature ; and his manner, like mercury, rose and fell in sympathy with the public sentiment—showing that our de Trows have their uses after all. It was the young man's first appearance in anything approaching society since his engagement had openly been broken off. He who had been so accustomed to the smiles of the world ! Ah ! curse the world and its puppets ! No one else should have the chance to cut him, and offering his arm to Mrs. Asher, he defiantly led her through the rooms, addressing no one, and by no one addressed.

The spirit of the old Latin Saturnalia, of which this species of entertainment lingers as a relic, was returning. With the advance of the evening the dancing be-

came more pronounced, and it was objected
that the dividing line between the great
and the *demi-monde* had not been strictly
observed in the sale of tickets. Certainly
people whose characters were question-
able began to appear, and the render-
ing of quadrilles insensibly to glide into
a style more peculiar to the *fêtes* of
Bougival.

Immediately after supper most of the
ladies I have mentioned departed; and,
what with the champagne and the Strauss
music the entertainment verged closely on
the indecorous.

Mrs. Asher and her companion lingered
till two o'clock. The strains of the music
still floated in her memory, and she
hummed the airs as she drove home through
the darkened streets. The vicomte was
still gloomy and preoccupied; consequently,
he failed to notice when he rang the bell
that the latch of her *porte-cochère* was
drawn back, and the door open by a quarter
of an inch. At the portals he left her; for,
she had insisted that the proprieties
be rigidly kept between them. Thus

Mrs. Asher entered alone, and the vicomte saw the dark doors close upon her.

His own lodgings were not far away; and, though still arrayed in costume, he resolved to walk, in order to get a breath of air. Yet some indefinable instinct held him, now looking back at the house, and again at his carriage disappearing in the gloom; for the moon had long since set, and the few lamp-posts scarcely illuminated the street. At last he started for his hotel. The music of her voice was in his ears, and the perfume of her lips on his as he walked on. He had gone about a hundred yards, when a figure detached itself from the darkness and approached him. It was not until the stranger drew quite near, that the vicomte recognized the uniform of a *sergent de ville.*

"Pardon; has monsieur just left No. 13?" inquired the officer.

"And what is that to you?" replied the vicomte brusquely.

"Because I am watching that house, and am directed to arrest anyone loitering about it."

"You are directed to arrest anyone loitering about that house?" replied the
vicomte in supreme surprise.

"Such are my orders, monsieur, unless
I am satisfied concerning their intentions.

"I am the Vicomte de Dindon. I have
just brought madame back from the ball,
and am returning to my hotel."

"Oh, pardon; I did not recognize monsieur at first. I know him well. I might
have supposed it was he who drove up in
that carriage; but it was so dark I could
not distinguish."

"And who gave you these orders?"

"They came from headquarters, monsieur. I suppose I may as well inform
monsieur. Indeed I do not know but it
is my duty to do so. It was in this way.
About three or four hours ago, a woman
describing herself as the maid of Madame
Asher arrived at the Mairie, and was
closeted with the *commissaire de police.*
After she had gone, I learned that she had
demanded protection for her mistress;
and asked that one, or, if possible, two
policemen should be immediately detailed

to patrol her house. What with the carnival and the extra force of men required at the ball, there was some delay in sending anyone here. I have been at my post less than an hour."

"It is very odd," replied the vicomte, " that no mention of this was made to me. If you will return with me, I will try to learn the cause of such a request."

They retraced their steps.

"It was probably because madame feared for her diamonds. This carnival has brought many thieves to the city."

"Perhaps so ; and yet, when I let madame in, the front door was unlatched. I quite forgot the circumstance till this minute."

"But it is closed now," said the *sergent*, pushing against the heavy portals ; " and it seems a pity to wake the household. Madame will have retired too."

"I suppose so."

"Therefore monsieur had better wait till the morning. I am to remain outside until daybreak."

The vicomte looked up at the house, from which not a ray of light shone.

"Well," he said at last, "I suppose I can leave things in your hands; but stay, what is that?" He stopped and listened.

"What is what, monsieur?"

"I thought I heard something like a subdued scream."

"I heard nothing."

"Hush! there it is again," whispered the vicomte.

"*Diable*, I think I heard it myself; besides, they are moving inside. Lights are beginning to show at the windows, as if something were happening. We must ring."

They rang—a loud peal; no answer. Again and again they pulled the iron handle of the bell rope.

"Where can the *concierge* be?" muttered the *sergent*.

"Knock on the door with the butt of your sword," cried the vicomte. "I am sure all is not well."

"*Diable*, why don't they come? I hear that scream again. Open! open in the name of the law!"

They try to force the portals; they hammer; they ring; thoroughly alarmed, they shout aloud for entrance. Lights are darting about within, as from lamps hurriedly borne past windows; but why, why does no one answer the summons? Then above them a casement is burst open, and a head emerging, a female voice cries aloud: "*Au secours! au secours!* they are murdering my mistress!"

"Assistance is here," shouted the vicomte in reply. "I, the Vicomte de Dindon—you know me—with the police. Open the door, in the name of God."

"I come—I come," was answered, and the head withdrew.

And now, between the confused cries above and below, there came through the opened window wild, agonizing screams—screams that turned the blood cold, and that pierced like as many knife-thrusts the night air. At last the door is opened by the woman. They follow her through the *porte-cochère* and into the house, where they find the servants, in the scantiest costumes, huddled together in the hall. "Cowards! they had not even the courage to let you in," cried their conductress.

"The assassin must have entered when I was away to the Mairie; he must have passed by that imbecile asleep in his chair," and she flung a contemptuous glance at a quaking footman.

"But hurry, hurry, or you will be too late. Upstairs—to her boudoir. You know the way, Monsieur le Vicomte; she is locked in."

"Follow me," cried the vicomte.

"On, on," cried the *sergent*, with his sword drawn; and they rushed up the stairs, which, as in spacious French houses, made a wide semicircular sweep to the upper floor. They had just reached this landing when the door of the boudoir was flung open and a tall, angular figure emerged.

So unexpected was the advent, so unusual the appearance, that for an instant they stopped as if an apparition were barring their progress. For, though wild and unkempt looking, there was something intensely pathetic in the gaze of the intruder—something even noble in his mien as he stood there in the uncertain light.

"Assassin ! assassin !" they shouted.

"She is dead," he answered. "But conscience is her only assassin. For months I have followed her ——"

"And why?" interrupted the vicomte.

"To try to wean her from her present life."

"Seize him !" cried the vicomte. "He must be a maniac."

"Yes, I am a maniac; for I supposed, if I could see her but once, I could explain the past."

They flock into the apartment from which the man has just emerged, and find her whom they seek, lifeless on the floor. The vicomte and her attendant drop on their knees beside her. "Turn on the lights—higher," he cried. "Someone go for a physician."

"No use—no use—all is over." It is the attendant who speaks; and then, bursting into tears: "Oh, Monsieur le Vicomte, this is the dispensation of God. It was the sight of her husband's face that she could not meet."

XXXIX.

"You could have knocked me down with a feather," cried the young Augustus to his Lucretia next morning, when discussing the occurrences of the past night with his wife. "You see, he turns out to be her husband, and he has been pursuing her over the world."

"O Percival, I fear you would never pursue your wife so enthusiastically."

"I am not a lunatic," retorted Mr. de Trow, with deeper irony than he intended, and then continuing, "but what principally strikes me about the whole affair is its eminent bad form. Imagine the class of life to which this creature must have belonged to have made it possible even in his aberration to have behaved as he did."

"But his great love, Percival, redeems his conduct. Do you know, I have sometimes felt that I could die happy if a man would only pursue me with a flaming sword."

"There was no flaming sword. He broke into her house to induce her to go home with him, and frightened her to death—that is all," retorted Mr. de Trow snappishly.

"But there was true romance in that man's soul. Yes, I insist upon it, Percival, misguided, misdirected, as his conduct may seem to you, there was his grand passion to redeem it. O Percival!" she volubly went on, "have you never felt that good form, as you call it, is the sepulcher of affection, and that tragedy, real, true, soul-inspiring, heart-thrilling tragedy, will find its grave in fashion? No, Percival, better a world of savages—better a land of Hottentots, where all go about with hats and sandals only—than the flabby, conscience-less callaosity of what modern society calls affection."

"What's callaosity?" inquired Mr. de Trow unappreciatingly.

"I can't explain exactly, Percival. In fact, I invented the word to express something I can only feel—for what you consider as quixotic strikes me as heroic, and I recognize that were all the world like you, Othello would never have drowned Desdemona."

"I suppose you mean that Othello would never have smothered Desdemona," replied monsieur in great disgust. "If you're going to quote, I'd advise you to get things straight."

"It's straightness robs modern society of its interest. Starch and prunella, stiff collars and primness—bah! I despise it. But I see you're angry; so, as I really don't want to quarrel with you, Percival, we'll change the subject. Pray tell me what they have done with this poor creature. Though all the world sneers, I can feel for him."

"He is where he ought to have been all along—in a strait-jacket. I hope he'll remain there," continued the gentleman stolidly. "It's a little too bad having a quiet town disturbed in such a manner and everyone's nerves shaken up so."

The lady sighed; then with a subtle difference of intonation, she pensively continued: "Of course, I'm deeply pained at this terrible event, and feel as sadly as any-one for this unhappy woman cut off so suddenly in her prime. But things being as they are, we must bow, Percival, to the inevitable ; consequently, there is a suggestion I should like to make—that is, if you promise me first that you won't consider it cold or unfeeling."

"I cannot very well promise you what I shall think of it till I hear what it is," replied Mr. de Trow with unanswerable logic.

"Well, my suggestion is that we should be on the alert to engage her cook. You know he was reputed the best *chef* in Paris, and I feel sure the applications for him will be without number."

"I have already done so," replied Mr. de Trow, with an air of conscious pride. "Immediately I heard of the occurrence, I sent around and concluded a bargain with him."

"That was truly considerate of you, Percival." Then, more sentimentally, "Do you know, Percival, I have ofttimes thought that there existed some subtle affinity between the hearts and the palates of men."

"Not a bit more than between those of women," interjected de Trow.

"And the very first person we must ask to dine," continued the lady, heedless of the interruption, "is the vicomte. Poor fellow—he must sadly need consolation. Go around to-day, this very morning, Percival, and leave your card. Be kind to him, Percival; cheer him up, and let him feel that he has friends at least in us," and through the lady's fervent imagination floated the idea that in the natural course of events the young man might take his place in the flock after all.

To do the vicomte justice, the blow was a severe one. He was one of the kind that nurtures grief and feeds on it. His gloomy mien, as he daily walked the Promenade des Anglais, invariably attracted attention.

"There is constancy for you—oh, if I had a lover like that!" and the speaker, the youthful wife of a crabbed old grocer, sighed with a sigh that might have inspired

Zola with the idea for a new realistic romance, or Ibsen with a fresh moral. Indeed, there was something especially *piquant* to the French imagination in the whole situation. What a beautiful picture too for other young men to model their lives on! Had he been already married his regret would have been regarded as commonplace, but now it was full of color, full of true nobility and of poetry. So the public sentiment toward the vicomte began to change, at least on the part of the women, and of the poorer classes of the people, who have this in common that they never take a middle course, but are always either stoning or worshipping their betters.

XL.

REFLECTIONS OF AN AMERICAN DIPLOMAT ON THE EVE OF HIS RESIGNATION.

AND what has become during all this interval of our good friend Judge Jackson? Why, simply he has been paying the too frequent penalty of a visit to the Eternal City. Having suffered from a severe attack of Roman fever, he is only now able to sit up and read the papers.

"Martha, let's go back to Dianapolis," he exclaimed one morning, throwing down the copy of *Galignani's Messenger*, which gave a detailed account of the events last recorded. "There's a purity and simplicity about life there that we look in vain for here. Indeed, what you once observed about our not fitting in here has lately appealed to me with more force than ever; and, if you're willing, I'll hand in my resignation at once."

The kindly face of the lady lighted up, and two tears shone in her eyes like sparkling rain drops in an April sky. She came and put her arms about her husband's neck.

"I have been very unhappy lately, Samuel, but I am now repaid by what you say. It isn't that I desire to cavil at European society. It isn't that I esteem myself above others, but I believe that each country is best for its own people to live in. Judging from what I've seen, those that live out of their own are too apt to acquire, if not the vices of the people they abide among, at least their follies; and, having broken all their own home ties, they never acquire fresh ones."

"Martha, you've put the case in a nutshell. Americans in Europe are Americans in exile. I might even add—the ministers and representatives we send out here are often in the same boat. The fact of the matter is with the development of American interests in Europe we ought to have a regularly trained diplomatic service.

I see things straighter now and Pettigrew is right in what he has always claimed. There'll be some terrible blunder committed one of these days from which the country

will suffer—I came near making one myself. Why if your going to build a wall
around your backyard—you don't confide
the job to a man who has never laid bricks.
No, Martha, the United States is destined to
play a pretty big part in the world and it's
only a matter of time before Washington
will see the matter in the right light. As
for me, however, this diplomatic business
would never have suited me. Even
now I long for the bustle and movement of home politics, and I feel that
I can no longer resist the temptation of
going and looking up that nomination to
the governorship. After that——"

"And after that, Samuel?"

"If you'll put down your ear, I'll tell
you a secret, Martha."

The lady did as she was bid. "And
after the governorship, there's the presi-
dency. I've known stranger things to happen than the one leading to the other."

"And would you be happier, Samuel, in
the White House?"

"Oh—it isn't for myself I am thinking
as much as for you."

"For me?"

"Yes, there'a an eminent fitness in your becoming the first lady in the land. For I confess I want to let the world see a specimen of perfect womanhood, and to enshrine in the hearts of future generations, with the name of Martha Washington, that of Martha Jackson—my wife!"

THE END.

www.ingramcontent.com/pod-product-compliance
Lightning Source LLC
Chambersburg PA
CBHW020926120726
47905CB00008B/2395